The smoke hit him first, its acrid smell thick in his nose.

Though his instinct was to yank open the cabin door, instead he touched the wall. Heat emanated from it, as did the crackle of flames.

He hurried back and woke Brianna. "Fire. We have to get out of here. Now."

There was no way out but to fight their way through the flames.

"Go," he ordered. "I'll be right behind you."

He wrapped her daughter in a blanket, hunched over Brianna and ran through the flames.

The cabin went up quickly, the flames eating the cedar siding with hungry bites of fire and fury.

"Someone set that fire deliberately. He could still be here."

Brianna pulled out the keys and they fought through the wind and snow to the truck.

With no time to relax when their assailant could be right behind them, Brianna sped down the slick mountain road. Suddenly, she hit a patch of ice. There was no time to even scream a warning as the truck spun out of control—straight to the edge of the mountain.

Jane M. Choate dreamed of writing from the time she was a small child when she entertained friends with outlandish stories complete with happily-ever-after endings. Writing for Love Inspired Suspense is a dream come true. Jane is the proud mother of five children, grandmother to ten grandchildren and staff to one cat who believes she is of royal descent.

Books by Jane M. Choate

Love Inspired Suspense

Visit the Author Profile page at LoveInspired.com.

ROCKY MOUNTAIN VENDETTA

JANE M. CHOATE

LOVE INSPIRED SUSPENSE
INSPIRATIONAL ROMANCE

LOVE INSPIRED® SUSPENSE

INSPIRATIONAL ROMANCE

ISBN-13: 978-1-335-58795-4

Rocky Mountain Vendetta

Copyright © 2022 by Jane M. Choate

For questions and comments about the quality of this book, please contact us at CustomerService@Harlequin.com.

Love Inspired
22 Adelaide St. West, 41st Floor
Toronto, Ontario M5H 4E3, Canada
www.LoveInspired.com

Printed in U.S.A.

And the Lord, he it is that doth go before thee; he will be with thee, he will not fail thee, neither forsake thee; fear not, neither be dismayed.
—*Deuteronomy* 31:8

To my dear friend Marian, who puts up with me,
encourages me and strengthens me.
What would I do without you?

ONE

A morgue had to be one of the coldest places on earth.

That was Gideon Stratham's first thought as he entered the morgue of Shadow Point, Colorado. His second was to wonder why he'd been summoned there.

When Nate Saxton, long-time friend and former colleague in the US Marshals Service, asked Gideon to meet him there, he had agreed immediately. Nate wasn't one to make such a request without reason.

Nate hadn't yet shown up, so Gideon looked around the room, with its cinderblock walls and trays of sterilized instruments. A stainless-steel gurney sat empty, mute evidence of what would shortly take place. The space had been ruthlessly organized and was immaculately clean.

For now.

Soon, he knew, there would be splatters of blood and other substances. He'd sat in on enough autopsies to understand the matter of unraveling death, though he'd never be comfortable with the sight. No surprise, considering he had seen more than his share of death when he'd been deployed as a SEAL.

An attendant sketched a wave at Gideon, and he acknowledged it with a nod.

When Nate showed up with a tray holding three coffees, Gideon raised an eyebrow. "When you said coffee, I thought you meant at Starbucks. What's with meeting in the morgue?"

Nate didn't rise to the bait. "Thanks for coming" was all he said. His expression was uncharacteristically grim, the usual glint of laughter in his eyes conspicuous by its absence.

The ME joined them at that moment. Doris Dunnaway could bench-press 250 pounds and not break a sweat. She was a no-nonsense woman who shot from the hip and expected others to do the same. He'd learned to both like and respect her during his time with the marshals. Those who attempted to shoehorn her into a one-size-fits-all slot were destined for disappointment.

She accepted the coffee with a brief nod of thanks. Her face as grim as Nate's, she led the way to the exam table where two attendants had placed the body. With a gesture from her, one pulled back the cloth draping the body.

Gideon drew in a sharp breath. "Judge Racine?" Now he understood why Nate had asked to meet here.

Doris nodded. "Yeah. Brought in last night."

Gideon had known the judge, who had a law-and-order reputation, for years. When he'd served as a US Marshal, he'd testified in the judge's courtroom on more than one occasion. The judge had subjected everyone who entered his courtroom to a gimlet eye, and was less than tolerant to anyone who wasted his time. He had been fair-minded, impartial and, most of all, just.

Two neat holes in his forehead, an execution-style murder, marred the patrician features. The ME pulled back the sheet a few more inches to indicate the *Y* cut. "I'm just starting, but it looks pretty straightforward. No surprises so far. The judge kept himself in good shape." Though Doris always kept her emotions in strict check, there was the slightest quaver in her voice. She cleared it with an impatient cough. "I testified before him more than once. He was a good man." She turned to give Gideon a fleeting smile. "Didn't expect to see you here, Stratham."

"Didn't expect to be here. It's good to see you, Doris, but I wish it was under different circumstances."

"Me, too." She didn't miss a beat and continued, "He was found in his car in the courthouse parking lot. Determining TOD is going to be tricky."

Time of death was dependent upon many factors, not the least of which was temperature. Temperatures had ranged from below zero to the low teens in the last several weeks. The courthouse's underground parking lot was bound to have been even colder.

"Can you tell us if the judge was killed where he was found?" Nate asked.

Doris shot him a reproving look. "You'll get what I have when I have it. Not a minute sooner." She made a shooing motion to Nate and Gideon. "Now get out of here and let me do my work." With that, she got back to the business of death.

Before they left, she looked up briefly, her gaze part mourning, part anger. "And find whatever lowlife did this to the judge. He didn't deserve this." Her voice softened, as did her eyes. "He didn't deserve this at all."

In the unheated corridor leading outside, the two men walked and talked.

Nate warmed his hands around the cup of coffee. "You know Rex Jameson has been released two months ago."

Gideon figured everyone in the state, maybe the country, knew of the notorious criminal's release from prison on a technicality. The man was a stone-cold killer, yet he'd gotten out when his lawyer had proven that a lab technician handling the evidence hadn't properly maintained the chain of custody, a stupid mistake that had set a murderer free.

The technician had been fired, but it hadn't changed what had amounted to a travesty of justice. Gideon knew the rules had been put in place for a reason, but he couldn't halt the surge of anger coursing through him.

"He's free to go about his business, just like you and me." Nate's voice held a sour note.

Gideon snorted. Aside from his criminal enterprises, Jameson's tentacles were far-reaching, with his fingers in every field of commerce.

Law enforcement agencies saw those so-called legitimate businesses as a way for Jameson to launder money, but they'd never been able to prove it.

"Do the police have eyes on him?" Gideon asked now.

"Not officially. It'd be considered harassment since he's not on parole. Or anything else."

It wasn't the first time Gideon had come up against the rule book. That was one of the reasons he'd left the marshals and taken a job with S&J Security/Protection. The job change had been a positive one, and he felt like he was making a real difference, helping people who were in trouble and had nowhere else to turn.

He and Nate reached the exit, a heavy steel door that required some muscle to open. The outside air blasted them with a fierce wind that blew down from the Rockies. Both men huddled deeper inside their jackets.

"Have you heard from Leah?" Nate asked.

So that's what this was about.

Not by a flicker of his eyes did Gideon show that the question had gotten to him. "She went off the grid the same time Jameson was put away."

"With good reason."

Leah Fuller had been a US Marshal, along with her husband, Jack. Both had worked the Jameson case, though on separate details since husbands and wives weren't allowed to work together. Jack and Gideon had been partners. On their last assignment, Jack had taken a bullet to the chest and had died on the spot.

Rationally, Gideon knew that Jack's death hadn't been his fault—Jameson had shot Jack point blank before Gideon could react—but he had a hard time convincing himself of it, another reason he'd left the marshals. He had shot Jameson, wounding him badly, but it hadn't brought Jack back. Jameson had recovered and stood trial, promising revenge on Gideon, two other officers, and Leah, who had orchestrated the takedown from the marshals' command post.

"Jameson will be coming for her," Nate said. "And for you." He lowered his voice, though there was one around. "We've got a mole."

"How do you know?"

"I don't *know*. Toria Callahan," he said, naming the chief marshal covering Colorado and other western states, "doesn't believe it. But I suspect it. We've lost two witnesses in the Jameson case in only two months. What does that tell you?"

Gideon absorbed the implications. New identities and locations for witnesses were generated by a proprietary algorithm. Only a few people had access to the code to the algorithm, much less the information itself. "Nothing good."

They reached their cars. "This is strictly off the record," Nate said, "but we need you. Someone has to get to Leah and protect her." He waited a beat. "If you don't want to get involved, I understand."

"I'll do it." Gideon had a very good reason to say no, but protecting Leah had been a nonstarter from the first. Something dark and protective rose within him at the idea of Jameson targeting Leah.

There was a lot of history between him and Leah, and he didn't want to dwell on what that history included—that he'd always had feelings for her. He'd never acted on them, but couldn't help feeling disloyal to his friend.

He didn't like the job he'd accepted. Didn't like it at all. But he had no choice. He had to protect

Leah. He couldn't leave her to the mercy of Rex Jameson. Nor could he leave her on her own. She'd been out of the game for too many years.

Leah was in danger. For Gideon, that said it all.

The crack of a high-powered rifle punctuated the stillness of the early morning.

Gideon and Nate both dove for the ground and belly-crawled to shelter behind a car. Weapons drawn, they peered over the hood of the car, ducking quickly when more shots filled the air.

There was no one Gideon would rather take fire with than Nate. He was as steady as they came and had proven himself over and over, first in the Navy SEALs and then with the US Marshals Service.

The heavy door burst open and two police detectives who were also at the morgue came running out. They drew their weapons but no more shots sounded. Gideon figured they must have scared away the shooter.

Gideon lifted an eyebrow. "Nothing like being shot at to drive a point home."

She was being followed.

Brianna Thomas knew it. More, she felt it. In her gut. The place that didn't put up with lies or self-deception. The certainty rattled around in her brain and refused to be denied.

She knew the signs well. Too well. Each was like a cold breath whispering over her face.

The nearly undetectable swish of a figure disappearing into a doorway. The hush of silence where there should be noise. The unmistakable sensation of the hair on the back of her neck prickling to attention.

Yes, she was being followed. Again. She'd known it since noon, when she'd walked Ruthie home from kindergarten. Now, in the small house she'd rented, she looked at her daughter playing with her cat, Miso, on the living-room floor. The quiet contentment that had been theirs for the last year was about to come to an end.

Brianna felt a desperate need to reject her suspicion, to talk herself out of the sense of foreboding that had overtaken her, but she couldn't give in to that luxury. Her child's life, not to mention her own, depended on what she did next.

As always, she was on her own to deal with it.

Still, the unfairness of it washed over her, causing her to want to trade lives with someone who wasn't being hunted by a convicted murderer. Her mind was still struggling to catch up to the idea that Rex Jameson had been released on a technicality. And despite how the news had grabbed the air out of her lungs, she would do what had to be done.

Ever since she'd heard of the court's decision

to release him from prison, she'd known this day was coming. She'd hoped she'd have a little more time, but now it was here.

Wasn't it enough that she'd changed her name and moved five times in the last six years? Wasn't it enough that she'd left the job she loved and, what's more, been good at, more than good at? Wasn't anything enough?

Apparently not.

Brianna did what she'd done before. She squared her shoulders and made plans, but she couldn't help heaving out a breath that was more resignation than resolve. It wouldn't be as easy to pull up stakes and move this time.

Ruthie had made friends in kindergarten. What's more, Brianna had made friends with another single mom. Friends were a luxury she hadn't allowed herself in the last few years.

Friends and library cards and a host of other things had been off-limits for her and Ruthie. Friends meant sharing bits and pieces of one's life. Library cards meant showing ID. How could she present ID when she wasn't even using her real name?

Leah Fuller had ceased to exist. She was Brianna Thomas now. And Suzanne and Rachel and Molly and Annie before that. As far as she knew, no one had tracked her down, but she couldn't count on that, so she had changed her name and moved to a new town every year.

For the last year, she and Ruthie had lived in Silverton, a small mountain community that had started life as a mining town. They were making a life for themselves here, a good life. She didn't want to leave it.

Get over it. Whining wasn't going to get her anywhere. She ought to know. She'd done enough of it in the past.

"We're going on an adventure."

Ruthie's eyes widened before understanding settled in them. Her small shoulders drooped. "We're moving again, aren't we?"

Brianna kept up the forced gaiety. "Yes. We're going somewhere new. Isn't that exciting?"

"I don't want to leave. I have a friend. A real friend. We play together at recess. Every day."

"I'm sorry, Ruthie. It can't be helped."

"You always say we should be fair. But you aren't being fair, making us leave."

Brianna didn't try to talk her daughter out of her feelings. Ruthie was right. It wasn't fair. Nothing in the child's short life had been fair, including having a mother who was constantly on guard.

"I want to stay here."

The five little words held a wealth of longing mixed with a good portion of mutiny.

"I want to stay, too," Brianna said with all honesty.

"Then why can't we?"

How did she argue with a child's logic?

"I'm sorry. It can't be helped." Her words came out more clipped than she'd intended. "I'm sorry," she said again. How could she explain to her five-year-old daughter that they had to leave the only real home she had ever known?

"I don't want to leave." A rebellious look took up residence in Ruthie's eyes, causing her to look fiercely stubborn.

"Ruthie, please." Brianna swallowed back her impatience and her grief. She paused for a moment, considering the word. Grief. Yes, she and Ruthie were both grieving for the coming loss. "Please try to understand—" She stopped herself. How could her tiny daughter understand what she was struggling to understand herself?

Ruthie folded her arms across her chest and stuck out her chin. Such defiance in such a small girl. With her little chin jutted out, she resembled Jack, Brianna's late husband. A lump lodged in her throat, and she had to swallow a couple of times to get rid of it.

Brianna stooped to hug her daughter. "I'm sorry." How many times must she say those words?

As many as it took.

But Ruthie wasn't having it. She pulled away and ran to her room. Brokenhearted sobs could be heard through the flimsy door.

Brianna wanted to sob as well, to pretend that she didn't have to uproot their lives. Again.

Instead, she sobered and went into Ruthie's room. The sight of her daughter lying on her bed, crying so hard that her tiny chest heaved up and down, nearly did Brianna in. She pulled Ruthie into her arms and was rewarded when her daughter didn't pull away.

They rocked back and forth together, Brianna singing a favorite song. When the sobs stopped, Ruthie looked up. "I'm sorry, Mommy. I didn't mean to get mad at you. But I really don't want to leave." A hiccupping sob accompanied the words.

"I know, darling. It's hard leaving friends."

"I've never had a real friend before, and now I have Lily. I don't want to leave her."

"Of course you don't." Brianna felt her own face fold up under the weight of her daughter's sorrow.

"Make it so that we don't have to leave," Ruthie said with a child's faith.

Brianna only wished it was so.

Unfortunately this was something she couldn't fix. Not if she wanted to keep her child safe. And keeping Ruthie safe was the only thing that mattered.

She turned to the task of preparing to leave. She wanted to be on their way in less than ten minutes. Fortunately she and Ruthie had go bags.

When she finished packing lunches and seeing to the needs of Miso, she called for Ruthie. "We need to be on our way."

The silence from her daughter's room grabbed her attention.

"Ruthie? Ruthie? Where are you?" Brianna stopped, struck by the strident voice that echoed off the walls. Surely that wasn't hers.

It was a game of hide-and-seek. That was all. There was nothing sinister about a little girl playing her favorite game, a game they'd played many times.

At the time, it'd seemed like a good idea, teaching Ruthie how to hide. But not now, especially when she looked to no avail in all of Ruthie's hiding places.

"Please, honey, come out. Mommy's getting worried."

Still, no sound.

She waited.

More silence.

When it grew oppressive, she methodically searched every place her daughter could conceivably hide. And a few places she couldn't.

Had Ruthie let herself outside? She knew the

rules. Knew that going outside by herself wasn't allowed.

But…

Brianna forced herself to think logically. Where would her daughter have gone?

More frantically now, Brianna went through the house a second time, a rising certainty that Ruthie wasn't there constricting her throat. With this search, she discovered that Ruthie's backpack was missing.

Where could she have gone?

Their small house wasn't on a busy street, a deliberate choice on Brianna's part.

Calling the police wasn't a possibility. There would be too many questions—questions to which Brianna had no answers.

"Please, Lord, help me find her. I can't lose her. I can't."

The prayer should have calmed her, but her terror was such that even calling upon the Lord failed to quiet her fear.

Surely her daughter couldn't have gotten too far. It wasn't possible for her little legs to have carried her any great distance.

Was it?

Brianna felt herself giving in to the fear that spewed like acid through her veins, and reined it in on a harsh breath.

She checked the narrow strip of grass that

separated their house from the neighbors'. She checked the postage-stamp-size front yard. When she didn't see Ruthie, she knocked on the door of her neighbors and explained that she was looking for her daughter and wondered if they had seen her.

They hadn't.

The older couple looked surprised, as she had never even introduced herself before. With a hasty apology for disturbing them, she ran down the street.

There. Two houses down, she spotted Ruthie.

A screech of brakes had her tensing, and she saw a car come to an abrupt halt, a man getting out of the passenger side. He held out a puppy. When Ruthie didn't make a move toward it, he made a grab at her, his fingers skimming her backpack. If he managed to really grab hold of it, he would have her in his grasp.

"No!" Brianna ran for all she was worth.

She was within two arms' lengths of her daughter when a shot pierced the mountain air. A heartbeat later, strong hands pushed her to the ground.

"Stay down."

Her eyes focused on the man above her. "Gideon?" How could that be? She hadn't seen Gideon Stratham since the trial six years ago.

"Stay down," he repeated. "I'll get her."

In a flash of motion, he caught Ruthie and rolled to the side, protecting her with his body while returning fire at the same time.

Brianna scuttled toward her daughter. "Mommy?"

She reached for Ruthie's hand and tucked it in her own. "It's okay," she murmured.

But it wasn't okay. It wasn't okay at all.

TWO

Gideon fought the glare of the sun off the newly fallen snow as he aimed his gun. It was a powerhouse of a weapon, but its reach wasn't made for a battle against a rifle meant for long-distance firing, such as the one he suspected they were up against.

Unless he missed his guess, the shooter was using a hoplite, an extremely accurate weapon that fired the 5.56 round, but he couldn't be certain. Nor could he be certain there was only one shooter. He sheltered both mother and daughter by hunching over them.

The brilliance of the sun worked in their favor as the shots narrowly missed them. Sirens screeched in the distance. When an engine rumbled, he figured the shooter was hightailing it out of there.

When several ticks of silence had passed, he said to Leah, "I think we're safe to move." He got up, then helped up Leah, who had her daughter clutched to her chest.

"Let's get out of here," he said, the unnecessary words sounding foolish. He could think of a hundred other things to say to the woman who had occupied his thoughts for the last six years, but right now he needed to get them away from the scene before they were detained for questioning. If Nate was right and there was a mole in the US Marshals Service and that Jameson had friends in various police departments, it made sense that a dirty cop or two might be involved as well. He couldn't risk hanging around.

She pointed to a small house tucked between two larger ones. Questions filled her eyes, but they would have to wait. Getting mother and daughter to safety took all his attention now. They ran toward the house and entered. It was barely bigger than a shoebox, but the homey touches made it inviting. A child's art hung above the sofa, and a basket of toys occupied one corner.

"How did you find me?" she asked.

"I remember you saying once that you liked small mountain towns. From there, it was just a matter of legwork."

"You were always good at what you did," she said.

"So were you, Leah."

"It's Brianna now."

"Right. We have to get out of here. Now."

She leveled a steady look at him. "Let's go."

"Just like that?"

"Just like that. We have go bags already packed." She pointed to two duffel bags sitting by the front door. "All I have to do is put Miso in her carrier and we're good to go."

"Miso?"

"Ruthie's cat."

A cat? What had he signed on for?

Protecting a woman, a small child and a cat in a deadly game of hide-and-seek from an enemy who didn't play by the rules. Fortunately, those were the kind of games he was good at.

Really good.

Gideon Stratham was not the most handsome man Brianna had ever laid eyes on, but he was one of the most appealing. With a tall frame that was on the rangy side and an unmistakable military bearing, he stood out in any setting with blue-black hair and eyes so dark that they appeared to be black.

Despite no longer being a member of the Navy SEALs or a marshal—she'd heard he'd resigned from the marshals shortly after she'd left—he wore an air of authority in the set of his shoulders and in his expression, one that said he was in charge, whatever the situation. When he said something, people listened.

What had brought him back into her life right now, she couldn't have said, but she was grateful. So very grateful.

Whoever was after her had nearly gotten to Ruthie. If that had happened, it would have been game over. She couldn't hold out against threats to her child. No parent could.

There was nothing she wouldn't do to protect her daughter, including letting herself be taken by a man bent on exacting six years of revenge on her.

"Who's he?" Ruthie demanded with a frown in Gideon's direction.

Brianna didn't blame her daughter for her suspicious attitude. She'd been raised to regard everyone with a distrustful eye. "He's a friend." Brianna didn't explain further. She was too anxious to get Ruthie to safety.

Gideon represented safety. The reasons as to why he'd appeared in her life at this moment could be sorted out later.

She made quick introductions between Ruthie and Gideon.

Ruthie continued to consider him warily. "You better be nice to Miso." She said it with a fierce glare.

Brianna put a protesting Miso in her carrier

while Gideon and Ruthie continued to stare at each other, mistrust on her daughter's face, bemusement on Gideon's. If Brianna hadn't known better, she'd have said that Gideon, ex-SEAL and ex–US Marshal, was intimidated by her little girl.

He hefted the bags and carrier while she grabbed Ruthie's left hand with one hand and the spare car seat she kept near the bags with the other. With only the briefest glance around what had been their home, Brianna pushed out a shaky breath and walked out the door.

She and Ruthie followed him to his car, a mid-size gray sedan designed not to attract attention. The blandness of it would have caused her to smile at any other time. Bland cars and nondescript clothes were the order of the day for US Marshals.

While she strapped the car seat in the back seat and then fastened Ruthie in it, he loaded the bags into the trunk and set the carrier beside her daughter. A plaintive meow said that Miso wasn't pleased.

Grateful as she was to get Ruthie and herself out of danger, Brianna couldn't help looking behind them as they put the small town that had been home for over a year in the rearview mirror.

Gideon was impressed at her readiness. Though he shouldn't have been. Leah had always been a top-notch marshal. It made sense that she had carried over those skills into her civilian life.

The little girl and a cat, no less, had surprised him. Nothing in the meager information he'd been able to gather on Leah—Brianna now— had prepared him for that. It put a different spin on things, making protecting her that much more difficult.

Despite the seen-better-days sweatshirt she wore, blond hair scraped back into a ponytail and worried eyes, she was as beautiful as he remembered.

He didn't fool himself into believing that Brianna was glad to have him here. She needed him. That was all. He'd do well to remember that. His thoughts raced ahead to what came next.

Leaving town was the first step. He had a place where they could stay. Now all that remained was getting out of town without picking up a tail.

He employed multiple surveillance detection routes, a trick he'd picked up in the SEALs when protecting high-value assets and honed during his stint in the marshals. The SDRs weren't infallible, but they could throw off most tails.

It was tough, if not impossible, to tail someone in a residential neighborhood. There wasn't sufficient traffic to hide in. It also meant that the vehicle trying to shake the pursuers had a harder time getting away. He made a series of turns, then reversed the order. No one following them that he could make out. He repeated the process on parallel streets. Whoever was after Brianna and Ruthie had probably gone to ground when the sirens had sounded and was now waiting until another opportunity presented itself.

"Nicely done," Brianna said.

"Thanks."

Once out of town, he got on the interstate and continued on that for thirty miles before turning onto a less traveled road that gradually narrowed as it wound its way through the foothills. They had a distance to go, and he wanted to get there before dark.

"You're very quiet," Gideon observed.

"And you're so talkative."

His lips quirked. "Neither one of us would make a good talk-show host."

She smiled at that. "You're right."

He glanced in his rearview mirror at her daughter. "Jack's daughter?"

Her gaze softened, and she nodded. "Jack died before I knew I was expecting. He never knew."

"I'm sorry."

"So am I." The three words held a wealth of regret and something else, something he couldn't identify. He couldn't worry over it now. He had more important things to consider, like how he was going to protect Leah—Brianna, he reminded himself—and her daughter without any backup.

They were silent for a bit before she said, "Ruthie and Miso and I come as a set."

He smiled. "I got that."

"How did you end up being the one to come for us? The last I heard you'd left the marshals."

"Nate Saxton sent me."

She was too savvy not to realize the implications of that admission. "There's a mole in the office," she said flatly.

He wasn't surprised that she had put the pieces together and come up with the answer. "That's Nate's take on it. He didn't want to put you in jeopardy by sending someone who might be dirty after you." A frustrated breath later, he added, "But Jameson's people still got to you. I almost blew it."

How had Jameson's men gotten to her before he did? He'd been working flat out to find Brianna since accepting the assignment a week ago. It hadn't been easy, following her trail from one small town to another while tracking her change of names.

"You got to us in time. I can never thank you enough. If something had happened to Ruthie…"

She didn't need to finish the thought for him to know how much she loved her daughter. It was in the softening of her gaze whenever she looked at Ruthie. It was in her voice when she spoke her name.

He'd never known a mother's love like that and found himself envious of the little girl.

"We'll keep her safe. I promise."

"You always did keep your promises." Her words had a wistful quality to them that had him wondering what she meant. She looked out the window. "Where are we heading?"

"To the mountains."

"I figured that. *Where* in the mountains?"

"A cabin I own. We should be safe there." At her doubtful look, he added, "It's not listed in my name. Nobody will look for us there."

She shivered, an involuntary reaction he knew was as much as from fear as from the cold. "As long as it's warm and nobody can find us, any place is good with me."

If he was still a believer, he'd have asked the Lord for His help. They were both going to need every bit of strength they could muster if they were to stay one step ahead of the man who wanted Brianna and her daughter dead.

THREE

"Mommy, I have to go. I have to go *now*."

The urgency in Ruthie's voice awakened Brianna with a start. Stiff from leaning against the car door, she stretched. "How long have I been sleeping?"

"A half hour." Gideon slid her a sideways glance. "You snore."

"Do not." She felt the color rise to her cheeks. "Maybe a little."

"Gideon's right," Ruthie said. "You snore. You woke Miso and me up."

"Oh, I did, did I?"

"Mommy, I really have to go."

Brianna turned to Gideon. "I think we'd better stop as soon as we can."

"There's a gas station coming up in a couple of miles," he said.

"Can you hold it for a few more minutes?" she asked her daughter.

"I don't know." The last word ended on a wail.

Gideon slanted a grin Brianna's way. "Don't worry. I'll drive faster."

Being swallowed up in his smile reminded her how much she'd liked him six years ago. And now? That didn't matter.

It couldn't.

Keeping Ruthie safe was all that mattered.

A few minutes later, they arrived at the gas station. Brianna and Ruthie hurried to the ladies' room and took care of business. Five minutes later, they met up with Gideon in the connecting convenience store, a much happier Ruthie in tow.

"Can we get a treat?" she pleaded. "Miso told me she was going to starve if she doesn't have something to eat."

"I think we can swing a treat," Brianna said with a smile for her daughter's tactics.

While Ruthie chose a candy bar and chips, Brianna looked for something a little more nutritious. She came away with a package of cheese and crackers and a bottle of water, along with a huge sack of cat litter and a box of plastic bags.

Gideon joined them, holding a grease-stained bag. "I picked up some burgers and fries at the grill."

So much for healthy.

Back in the car, they chowed down on the fast food.

"Thanks," she said, unabashedly licking crumbs

from her fingers. "I didn't realize how hungry I was."

After disposing of the trash, they were on their way again.

Gideon had seen to everything, including taking care of Miso's needs, helping her put cat litter in gallon-size bags for easier access.

How foolish to have brought a cat along, but there had been no question that they would take Ruthie's pet with them. Miso was family.

Gideon had been great throughout the trip, she thought, but she wasn't comfortable relying on him. For the last five years, she alone had been responsible for herself and Ruthie.

What would happen when he was no longer around? Brianna knew that nobody stuck around forever. She couldn't afford to rely on him. The sooner she accepted that, the better off she and Ruthie would be.

She couldn't remember the last time someone had cared about what happened to her. She was tough because she'd had to be.

And she was okay with that. But she couldn't deny that it felt good having someone to watch her back, if only for a short time.

Her bladder empty and her tummy full, Ruthie was happily chatting.

"Gideon and I talked a lot. We're best friends

now. Well, except for you and Miso and Lily. You'll always be my first best friends."

Brianna twisted around as far as the seat belt would allow to look at her daughter. "So you and Gideon are best friends now? Is that right?"

Ruthie nodded. "Gideon said it was all right to take Miso out of her carrier and hold her on my lap."

It was Brianna's turn to slide him a glance. "That was nice of him."

"Miso was lonely."

"Oh."

"She was making that sound she does when she's sad," Ruthie added.

Brianna let her gaze rest on Gideon. "Thank you," she said in a quiet voice. "For everything."

"Gideon said we're going to a log cabin and that I can roast marshmallows in the fireplace. We've never had a fireplace before. I can't wait."

Ruthie's excitement knew no bounds at the prospect, and Brianna gave a silent prayer of gratitude that her daughter was no longer despondent over having to leave their home.

Brianna allowed herself a sad smile. Her daughter was once again her happy self, unaware that a relentless killer was after them both.

When she spotted a pickup truck following them, she tensed. Pickups weren't uncommon, but the way this one stuck to their tail caused her gut to clench.

He didn't slow down, didn't speed up, just kept a steady pace behind them.

Maybe it wasn't anything more sinister than a farmer delivering feed to an outlying pasture. She hoped that was the case.

Seconds later the vehicle closed the gap between them. She made out two men. How had they managed to find them?

How?

There was no way someone could have planted a tracking device on his car—Gideon had checked the vehicle before they started off.

Her seat belt tightened when the truck rammed them from behind. When it hit them again, she braced herself.

Okay. Lines had been drawn.

"Mommy?" Ruthie ventured, her voice a high-pitched squeak.

"It'll be all right." Brianna turned her attention to Gideon. "Tell me what you want me to do."

"Are you as good as you once were at taking out a moving target?"

"Yes." She had kept up her shooting skills, knowing that someday she might need them.

He eyed her purse. "I assume you're carrying."

"Always."

"Think you can hit the engine?"

"Watch me." She pulled a Walther from her purse and, after rolling down the window, took aim. Two shots fired in rapid succession hit the engine block.

Steam exploded from the engine.

She made a sound of approval, but her satisfaction was short-lived.

They'd stopped their enemies. For now. But what about the next time? And the time after that? How long could they keep this up?

"That was close," she said.

"Too close."

His words were so low-pitched that she had to strain to catch them, telling her that Gideon was as worried as she was.

She glanced at Ruthie, saw the fear in her daughter's eyes. She firmed her jaw. Nothing was going to hurt Ruthie. Nothing.

They weren't going to reach the cabin by night.

Traveling with a small child and a cat meant extra stops along the way. Numerous restroom breaks, plus those for snacks, ate away the time. He could keep going indefinitely, but he knew Brianna and Ruthie were growing tired.

"What do you say we stop for the night?" Gideon asked.

From the grateful look Brianna sent him, he knew he'd made the right decision.

The nondescript motel promised free Wi-Fi and privacy. Gideon didn't care about the former, only the latter. After renting adjoining rooms, he parked at the back of the motel and carried Ruthie, who was drooping by now, inside.

He then raided a vending machine and brought back sandwiches and drinks to the room. After a hasty supper, they turned in for the night. He kept the door separating the rooms open. Though he respected Brianna and Ruthie's need for space, he wasn't going to close the door. He needed to be able to hear any noise that could represent a threat.

Their enemies had proven that they were a step ahead of them. No matter how he played it, he couldn't figure out how the men had found them. He was certain they hadn't been tailed. Nor did he believe that their pursuers had stumbled upon them accidentally.

It didn't add up.

He emptied his pockets, including several pairs of flex-cuffs, which frequently came in handy.

He dozed, but the light sleep he'd drifted into was broken by the murmur of voices outside. Silently, he slipped into the adjoining room.

Apparently Brianna had heard the voices, for she was up as well. "Someone's out there," she whispered.

"I know."

A splinter of glass later, a flash-bang filled the room with smoke. Gideon plucked Ruthie from the bed and sprinted through the open door to the next room, hoping the bad guys didn't know about the second room.

Brianna followed, Miso and their duffel bags with her.

He didn't turn on the light. Instead, he handed Ruthie to her, then pointed to the bathroom. "Stay in there."

"Where are you going?"

"To slow them down."

She didn't like that—he could see it in her eyes—but what choice did she have? She couldn't leave Ruthie alone to help him.

"Take care of yourself." Her voice was only a whisper, but the urgency in it came through loud and clear.

"Always."

After ripping off a shirtsleeve and tying it around his mouth and nose, he crept back into the first room. He figured the men outside were waiting for him and Brianna and Ruthie to surrender to the smoke and stumble out of the room, helpless and disoriented.

Well, he'd give them what they wanted. With a twist.

Hiding behind the doorframe, he flung open the door with one hand. A barrage of gunfire ensued. In the resulting cacophony of sound, he broke the window and fired out of it, taking out first one man and then a second.

He ran back into the room, where Brianna and Ruthie were waiting. "Let's go. We don't know if they have friends in the area."

Belongings in hand, they exited the room. While he kept watch, weapon at the ready, Brianna strapped Ruthie in her car seat, placed Miso's carrier next to her and climbed in the passenger seat.

The sudden quiet after the sound of gunfire had people cautiously opening their doors and peering around. A siren wailed in the distance.

Gideon didn't want to wait around for questions.

Cops didn't like people shooting up public establishments. He had no doubt that he'd be held at least until it was established that he wasn't the villain of the scenario, and, by that time, their enemies would have ample time to bring in reinforcements.

The sky remained dark as he drove out of the parking lot at a sedate pace. Several police cars, along with two ambulances, passed them on their way to the scene of the shooting. He hoped that he, Brianna and Ruthie looked like a vacationing family getting an early start on their day's travel.

"Don't get too comfortable," Gideon warned. "We're going to change cars soon."

"I guessed as much." Brianna glanced over her shoulder to check on Ruthie, who hadn't made a sound during the shooting or the scrambling exit from the motel room. "It's all right, Ruthie."

"I know, Mommy."

"She's been so brave," Brianna said in a hushed voice, "but she's too little to have to be brave all the time. I did this to her."

"You're too smart to believe that."

"Am I? I was the one who had to be a US Marshal. I was the one who orchestrated the raid against Jameson, even though I wasn't part of it. Maybe if I'd been content to stay at home, to be the kind of wife Jack wanted…" She didn't finish, leaving Gideon to wonder what she'd meant by the last part.

The desperation in her voice cut straight to his heart. It didn't take much deduction power to guess that she felt she had no one to turn to. He recalled that her parents had died overseas while serving in the Peace Corps before she'd joined the marshals. She and Ruthie were alone.

Except for him.

He was close enough that he could reach for her hand and take it in his own. But he didn't.

His resolve to keep mother and daughter safe hardened. Gun-toting men coming after a woman and a child didn't sit well with him. It didn't sit well at all.

FOUR

Brianna had learned to recognize the Lord's tender mercies wherever and whenever she could. So when she turned her head and saw that Ruthie had popped a thumb in her mouth and was now sleeping peacefully after the hurried exit from the motel, she gave a silent thanks.

She agonized over what constantly running was doing to her daughter. It wasn't enough that she protect Ruthie from that danger; she had to protect her from the fallout as well. She'd been too young for the first several years of her life to understand why she and her mother had to keep moving from town to town, from house to house. Now that she was older, she was beginning to understand that they had moved because bad men might find them.

Miso peered at Brianna through the mesh of the carrier. "We'll keep her safe." If she hadn't known better, she would have said that the cat nodded its agreement.

They drove for forty-five minutes until Gideon pulled off at a small used-car lot. She watched as he zeroed in on a bored-looking salesman. After a few minutes of negotiation, Gideon followed the man into a shack that might have been an office and reappeared shortly with a set of keys.

They transferred Ruthie, still asleep in her car seat, Miso and their bags, and within five minutes they were on their way again, this time in a ten-year-old minivan that screamed "soccer mom." Brianna would have laughed at the irony of an ex–Navy SEAL driving a minivan if their circumstances hadn't been so grim.

She flicked a droll look Gideon's way. "Who'd think to look for us in this?"

The corners of his mouth turned up in a wry grin. "No one, I hope. If my buddies from the teams saw me in this, they'd never let me live it down." His expression sobered. "Maybe this will slow down whoever's on our trail."

"Let's hope." She worked up her courage to ask the question that had been nagging at her from the beginning of the journey. "How do they keep finding us? It's like we have some kind of spotlight on us that's leading them right to us."

"I wish I knew." He sounded as perplexed and frustrated as she felt.

"No one had the opportunity to plant anything

in our bags," she said, thinking aloud. "I'm sure of it."

"I think you're right, but somehow they know what we're going to do practically before we do."

"I've been thinking about yesterday," she said, "when they tried to snatch Ruthie. Why do that if they were trying to kill me?"

"I don't think they were trying to kill you," Gideon said in the tone of someone who had been thinking things through and had reached a conclusion. "I think they were trying to slow you down so that you couldn't get to Ruthie in time. Once they had her, they knew you'd surrender."

"Jameson wants me dead. He made that abundantly clear at the time of the trial. Why try to take me alive?"

"Maybe you have something he wants."

"What?" She was genuinely puzzled. "I don't have anything valuable."

"Something you *know*?" Gideon suggested.

She lifted a shoulder in a helpless shrug. "I don't know anything. Nothing that would help Jameson, at any rate."

He glanced at her and frowned. "You look tired."

"No more than you do." But the interrupted night of sleep was catching up with her. She tried to stifle a yawn, but it broke through, anyway. "Sorry about that."

"Don't be. Close your eyes for a while. You've earned a rest. We're going to take a roundabout route to the cabin. If someone is tailing us, I want to know sooner rather than later."

"What about you?"

"I don't need rest."

It was a lie, and they both knew it, but Brianna was too tired to call him on it and didn't fight it when her eyes slid closed. Sleep beckoned. Just as she was about to give in to it, a vicious bump from behind startled her awake.

The icy roads plus a heavy hit from the rear sent the minivan swerving toward the edge of the road, the slick surface putting them on a deadly path to the bank, which fell in a steep drop-off.

Gideon didn't fight the vehicle's slide but turned into it and was able to maintain control, but that didn't mean they were out of trouble.

Far from it.

As the tires fought for purchase on the treacherous road, he fought to hold a steady course as the muscular-looking pickup rammed the minivan again.

The minivan lacked the power to outrun the truck. This vehicle was designed for safety, not speed. And while safety was all well and good, right now he needed to get them out of there.

He'd worry over how their enemies found them—again—later.

In the rearview mirror, he saw Ruthie stretching. He heard the question in her voice when she said, "Mommy?"

"It's okay, honey," Brianna returned.

"Miso was a little scared, but she's not anymore."

"That's good. Gideon?" Her tone held no panic, but the tension was clear.

The increasingly heavy snowfall caused the windshield wipers to work double time and gave him an idea. "I have a plan, but you're not going to like it."

"Try me."

"I want you to take the steering wheel. I'm going to give our friends a little surprise."

She didn't hesitate. "Let's do it."

He appreciated that she didn't ask questions, as he wasn't sure he was up to explaining what he had in mind. Even as he went over the plan in his mind, it sounded impossible to pull off.

It wasn't easy to switch seats, as she slid under him and he climbed over her, but they managed. He then scrabbled into the back seat, folding up his long legs to squeeze through the narrow space.

Earlier, he'd helped Brianna put cat litter in gallon-size plastic bags and found them in the bag of Miso's supplies. If he could throw a sack of litter at the windshield of the truck, it would cling to the wipers, slowing their speed, maybe even stopping them altogether.

What could possibly go wrong?

"You're going to *what*?" Brianna asked when he told her what he had in mind. "You won't be able to hit the windshield from this distance."

"If you hold the speed steady, I think I have a shot. We don't have many choices."

"What happens if the driver decides to speed up and run us off the road before you can throw the litter?"

"Show a little faith." The words nearly choked him, because he had let go of his faith long ago. Talk about a hypocrite, but right now he needed Brianna to believe in the plan. "Keep as close to the truck as possible without letting it hit you." He knew he was asking the impossible.

"I'll do my best."

He rolled down the window, wincing as frigid air blasted in, and hung out as far as he could. When he was lined up with the truck, he threw the bag of litter. His aim was sure, and the litter hit the windshield square on. The bag exploded and the escaping litter clung to the wipers, clogging them up until they crawled to a stop.

The truck veered to the right, then to the left, before finally running off the road completely and into a tree. Smoke steamed from the engine, signaling that the vehicle would be out of commission for some time.

Gideon allowed himself a small smile of satisfaction. "That should slow them down for a little while. You okay to keep driving?"

"I'm fine."

"Then let's get out of here."

Nimbly avoiding Ruthie and Miso, he climbed back over the seat and settled in the passenger side.

"Better buckle up," Brianna said. "The roads are growing slicker." She slid a glance his way. "That was a pretty neat trick."

"Thanks. If it gets them off our tail, I'll be satisfied."

"It's okay to close your eyes if you need to," she said. "You've been going flat out for hours."

Gideon grunted. "Maybe I will."

He let the vehicle's steady speed lull him into a relaxed state. He couldn't afford to let down his guard, not when Brianna and Ruthie were depending upon him, but maybe it wouldn't hurt to rest.

Just for a minute. No more.

Brianna knew Gideon had to be exhausted. She doubted he'd gotten much, if any, sleep at the motel. He'd kept her and Ruthie safe by drawing the fire of the two men and then taking them out.

She recalled how he'd handled himself as a marshal. Quiet and methodical, he never drew attention to what he did. Unlike her husband. Jack had always had to be in the limelight, demanding it if it wasn't shone upon him sufficiently. In the end, it seemed that no amount of praise or flattery could appease his ego. He needed those things the way others needed oxygen.

"Mommy?" Ruthie's voice startled Brianna out of her musings.

"Hmm?"

"Is Gideon asleep?"

"I think so."

"Good," Ruthie said with satisfaction. "I think he was tired. He's good at keeping the bad men from getting us, isn't he?"

"Yes, he is." Brianna thought of how he'd put himself in harm's way over and over to protect her and Ruthie.

"I'm glad he's my friend. Is he your friend, too, Mommy?"

Was he? Brianna wasn't sure. They were friendly with each other. But friends? She feared there was too much history between them for real friendship.

"Can we play a car game?" Ruthie asked, not waiting for Brianna's answer.

"Sure. What do you want to play?" They'd had lots of experience in playing car games with all the moves they'd made in the past years.

"Why don't we do the one where I say a word and then you say a word that rhymes?"

It was a favorite game, and Brianna was happy to comply.

"Glass," Ruthie said.

"Grass."

"Cat."

"Hat."

The routine answers soon grew boring, though, and Ruthie yawned. "Bad men chasing us makes me tired," she said. "Does it make you tired?"

Her daughter had a way of reducing complicated things to their simplest components. "Very tired."

"I'll help you stay awake." But when she gave another yawn and her eyelids drooped, Brianna knew her daughter was down for the count.

"Thank You, God," Brianna said in a prayer of gratitude. "Thank You for the gift of this child." She didn't deserve the wonder that was Ruthie, but she was forever grateful for her.

More than ever, she appreciated the Lord's faith in entrusting Ruthie to her. She prayed she could fulfill His belief in her.

She kept the speed at an even pace. No sense in drawing attention to themselves by speeding. When two SUVs turned onto the highway, Brianna kept them in sight through her rearview mirror.

Something about the way that they kept pace without coming too close set off an alarm in her.

SUVs weren't uncommon in the Rockies. Their rugged styling and heavy-duty suspensions made them perfect for the rough conditions frequently encountered in the mountains, but these vehicles stood out. They had larger-than-normal tires and what looked like bigger engine blocks beneath the elongated hoods. If she was to describe them, she'd have said they were hunting for bear.

"You made them," Gideon said, letting her know he'd been awake for some time.

"It was hard not to."

"What are you going to do?" he asked.

"This."

She turned off the highway, onto a narrow country road, and wasn't surprised to see the matching vehicles turn off, too.

The road wasn't meant for high-speed chases. She should have slowed her speed accordingly, but she couldn't afford to do so. Soon she found what she was looking for: a lane where scrub pine and other vegetation nearly concealed the entrance.

Such lanes were common along country roads, the result of off-roading enthusiasts who challenged themselves and their vehicles to navigate rough terrain. Right now, she could only give thanks that some intrepid ATV driver had decided to test himself and forge a new path. A slight bend in the road obscured her move from the SUVs following.

She killed the engine and prayed that her turn hadn't kicked up any snow to alert the men behind.

The SUVS chasing them missed the road and sped on by. By the time they realized they'd been duped, she planned to be far away. She needed to get back to the highway and put some distance between her and Gideon and Ruthie, and the men driving the SUVs.

Relief poured through her, but it was short-lived as a pickup with a crew cab and elongated truck bed came barreling toward them. She wasn't surprised at the number of lackeys Jameson had on his payroll.

He'd run one of the biggest criminal organizations in the West before he'd been sent to prison, and though that organization had been largely dormant during the last six years, he had apparently started it up again.

The truck obviously intended to run them off the road. It was a game of chicken. And Brianna was going to play.

She held her course. With the conversation with Gideon about whoever was after her not wanting her dead fresh in her mind, she intended to call the driver's bluff.

"Let's see what you've got," she murmured.

She didn't veer from her course. When impact seemed imminent, the other driver swerved, sending his vehicle down a steep ditch. The resulting crash and clanging of metal on rock sounded through the winter air. Most people would stop and look. Not Brianna.

She kept going.

Gideon gave a low whistle. "That was some driving. Remind me not to play chicken with you. I'd lose. Big-time."

She let out an unsteady breath. "I was shaking in my boots," she admitted.

"You didn't let on."

"I was too busy not blinking."

Gideon was in awe of the kind of courage it had taken for Brianna to hold steady upon seeing the pickup move inexorably toward them, knowing that their lives had depended upon what she did next. He marveled at her skill and daring.

He'd always known she was a first-rate marshal. What he hadn't known was that she was completely fearless.

He glanced at her, saw the pulse hammering at her neck, the tension in her knuckles as she gripped the steering wheel. No, that wasn't so. She had been afraid. Not for herself, but for Ruthie. That made what she'd done even more remarkable, to have acted so decisively despite her fear. "You're something else," he said. "I don't know many people who could have done what you did."

"I'm just a mother trying to protect her child. You've heard of the mama-bear syndrome?" At his nod, she said, "That's me. I'm a mama bear. No one hurts my child. No one."

He'd met a fleet admiral who lacked the resolution that this woman possessed.

Her words caused a wave of envy to roll through him. His mother had never tried to protect him, especially not from his stepfather. He pushed the painful memories from his mind and focused on what Brianna was saying.

"We better keep moving before another one of these goons finds us." Her eyes grew troubled. "How do they keep finding us? *How?*" Frustration filled the last word, resonating with his own.

She'd asked the question before, just as he had. Neither one of them had been able to come up with an answer.

"When we stop, we'll go through every bit of our stuff. There can't be a tracker on the minivan since we switched vehicles."

They continued heading north, until he suggested they stop for a break.

As though on cue, Ruthie awakened at that moment. "Mommy, I'm hungry."

"That seals it," Gideon said and pointed to a sign for a fast-food place.

Brianna pulled off the highway. Minutes later, they were devouring bacon, egg and cheese biscuit sandwiches.

"Mommy, can we have these every morning?" Ruthie asked, having finished her sandwich and looking like she could eat another.

Brianna sent him a now-see-what-you've-done look. "Probably not. Too many would be no good for you. But this is a special occasion."

"Because bad men are chasing us," she said, her words too wise for a small child.

"That's right."

But Ruthie had already returned to eating the fried potato cake that accompanied the sandwich and slurping juice from a juice box.

What did it say about the child that she so matter-of-factly accepted bad guys chasing them as her reality? It troubled him, as it no doubt troubled Brianna. It must tear her apart to know that her little girl had become so accustomed to the idea of men with guns hunting them that she could utter the words without any inflection of fear.

"Mommy, I have to *go*," Ruthie said. "Right now."

He smiled at the picture the girl made, unicorn backpack slipped over her shoulders, as she and Brianna made a trip to the restroom. While they attended to that, Gideon checked their belongings, looking for any devices that could lead their pursuers to them. He went over the duffel bags, the cat carrier, even the sacks of cat litter.

Nothing.

Could it just be good fortune on the part of Jameson's men that they were in the same area as Gideon, Brianna and Ruthie, and had stumbled upon them?

Even as he asked himself the question, he shook his head. He didn't believe in coincidences.

With him at the wheel, they started on their way once more. They needed to get off the roads where they had been so easily spotted. He wouldn't rest easy until they were tucked inside his cabin. No one outside of the man who had sold it to him knew of its existence or location.

During his time as a marshal and as an S&J operative, he'd received his fair share of threats. The opportunity to own a cabin that was totally off the radar had been too appealing to pass up, and he'd scraped together the money to buy it.

They would be safe there. If he had his way, no one would ever scare Ruthie again.

FIVE

Gideon had never brought anyone to his cabin before, not even his colleagues at S&J, who were the closest thing he had to family. What did it say, he wondered, that he'd brought Brianna and Ruthie and Miso here?

The secluded valley, tucked in the craggy Rocky Mountains, held a kind of peace rarely found in the outside world.

Brianna's eyes widened as she took in the large cabin, barn and two outbuildings. "I was expecting a tiny cabin in the woods, a little rough around the edges. This is—" she spread her arms "—gorgeous."

"Hardly gorgeous. But it does have running water," he added, tongue in cheek.

"It's breathtaking."

He hadn't thought about it much. Seeing it now through another's eyes had reawakened him to the beauty of the setting, the towering pines that marched like sentinels across the back edge of the property, the backdrop of mountain and sky, the cabin itself built from planked cedar that had aged to silver. The fading light as dusk set in coated the landscape with a soft glow, turning the snow to a pale pink that disguised the treachery of the heavy drifts and freezing temperatures.

"I like it." He thought about his life, the changes he'd make if he had a family. Time at the cabin. Time together. Just…time. "I don't get up here much."

It was a throwaway remark, but it was all he could come up with. Thoughts about family had scrambled his mind.

What did he know about being part of a real family? His father had died in an industrial accident when Gideon was only six, and shortly afterward his mother had married a man who took every opportunity to belittle her and to let Gideon know that he was in the way.

Gideon hadn't understood why his mother had married such a man but had come to the conclusion that she'd needed someone to take care of her. She'd died the year he graduated high school, and he hadn't looked back.

Until now.

Something about being with this mother and daughter was tugging his thoughts to unfamiliar places, leaving his feelings for Brianna more conflicted than ever.

"I'd spend every moment I could get away here. It must be glorious in the fall."

"It is." He pictured it as it had been a few months earlier, the trees so bright with color that they looked like a child's paint box, the mountain air green-apple tart. He'd like to bring Brianna and Ruthie back here for the next autumn, and imagined Ruthie's pleasure in stomping through leaves.

His train of thought startled him. Where had *that* come from?

"Thank you for bringing us here," Brianna said, "and sharing it with us."

"We should be safe here. I hope."

Some of the pleasure in Brianna's eyes died. He wanted to yank back the words that reminded her of why they were here, but he let them stand. They both needed to keep in mind the danger facing them.

To let down their guard for even a short while could prove fatal.

Brianna told herself she was grateful for Gideon's reminder of why they were at the cabin. Because a killer was after them. For the smallest of moments, she'd allowed herself to forget that and had just appreciated the unspoiled beauty of the setting.

It was time to get back to business. She parked in front of the cabin.

"I'll move the minivan into the barn once we get settled," he said.

She braced herself for the cold and hunched her shoulders against the blast of frigid air when she opened the door. Stuffing her hands deeper into her pockets, she gazed about, trying to get her bearings. The cabin sat nestled in the pocket of a valley seeming to slumber under a fresh coating of snow.

The wind, whipping through the soldier-straight pines, carried the scent of winter. And though she appreciated the mountain air, she huddled deeper into her jacket and wished she had something warmer.

If she hadn't been freezing and worried over keeping Ruthie safe, she'd have wanted to explore. Instead, all she could think about was getting her child inside and getting both of them warm and fed.

Brianna started to lift Ruthie from her car seat, but Gideon nudged her aside. "Let me."

He scooped Ruthie into his arms and cradled her to him.

Brianna watched the care with which he sheltered her daughter from the cold, huddling over her to protect her from the wind. Tears stung her eyes. It was the wind, she told herself—nothing to do with the gentleness he showed toward Ruthie.

After keying in a code to the door, he carried her inside, Brianna following with Miso.

"Everything's clean," he said. "I have a caretaker who sees to things. He also stocked the cabin with food and whatever else I could think that we needed."

Ruthie didn't waken, only sighed, and popped her thumb into her mouth once more as he carried her to a bedroom.

Brianna took a throw folded at the foot of the bed and placed it over Ruthie, then leaned down to brush a kiss across her cheek. "She's had to put up with so much in her life that sometimes I forget she's just a little girl."

"She's got a lot of spunk for being five years old." Gideon's smile invited her to agree.

"You're right about that," she said and reluctantly returned the smile with one of her own.

"You've done a good job with her."

"Thank you." And this time the smile didn't come so hard.

After retrieving their bags, Gideon drove the minivan to the barn. When he returned, he found Brianna standing at the stove.

"I heated up a can of soup," she said.

"Sounds good."

Within a few minutes, she filled bowls with

the surprisingly good soup. They ate in companionable silence.

"This will be over soon," he promised and then berated himself for the patently false hope the words were supposed to provide. The truth was, he had no idea when it would be over. No one did. All he could do was try his best to keep mother and daughter safe.

Apparently she recognized the statement for what it was, because the look she sent him was one of disappointment.

He dipped his head. "Sorry. That was a dumb thing to say."

"You're right. It was."

He pushed away from the table, gathered up the dishes and placed them in the dishwasher as she wiped off the counters and table. Together, they made short work of the cleanup.

"This is a far cry from my vision of a cabin in the woods," she said, gesturing to the microwave, dishwasher and other amenities. "How did you find it?"

"A friend was moving out of state and asked me if I was interested. He agreed to let me keep it in his name. It makes a good getaway. It's not fancy, but it suits me." He gestured to the sitting area. "We need to talk."

The comfortable atmosphere they'd enjoyed while eating the simple meal had disappeared, leaving a heavy presence of things that needed to be said.

The wary look she sent him told him she understood. She took a seat on the sofa, while he sat at an angle from her in an overstuffed chair.

If they didn't ease the tension between them, the days spent at the cabin were going to be a long stretch of time. He had to do something.

"Jameson and his cohorts are going to keep coming after us. I can't make it—" he made a defeated gesture "—go away. I wish I could. In the meantime, we have to live with each other."

He gave her a steady look and said, "We have a history, which, in my experience, can make things awkward." Awkward in that he had been her deceased husband's partner and she probably blamed him for his death. Awkward in that just looking at him no doubt brought up painful memories that they both wished could stay buried. Awkward in that he'd had feelings for her six years ago and those feelings had only grown. What was he supposed to do with them? Stuff them away and hope they didn't pop out at an inconvenient time?

Jack had saved his life more than once, and Gideon had returned the favor. Except for that last op, when everything had gone wrong. And his partner had died in Gideon's arms.

He wouldn't—couldn't—forget that night.

How could he forget when Jack's blood had stained his hands and clothes? And when he had looked at Jack's widow standing beside him at the funeral, slim shoulders straight, chin lifted in a resolute pose?

With a supreme effort of will, he forced the images from his mind and concentrated on the present.

"I suggest we put it behind us and focus on keeping you and Ruthie safe."

Her nod was as crisp as his words. "My thoughts exactly."

Her agreement, though, was negated by the weary look that crept into her eyes. Empathy swelled in him at what she must be going through. She had to be exhausted. They'd put in two extremely long days already.

That realization, along with the slight slump of her shoulders, made him long to give her a hug, but he suspected it would not be well received, so he kept his hands at his sides.

She stood. "I'm going to check on Ruthie, see if I can wake her up long enough to eat something, and then get ready for bed myself."

He thought of the obvious love between mother and daughter and the promise he had given to protect them both.

Could he do it?

With that, he set his jaw. He was all in.

SIX

Brianna stared at herself in the bathroom mirror. There were times when she gazed into a mirror and didn't recognize the face staring back at her. Had her mouth always been so drawn, her eyes so narrowed, her expression so guarded?

No, not always.

But the last six years had stitched her features into those of a woman who had forgotten how to smile. Only Ruthie had saved her from becoming a total recluse. Her little girl's laughter and sheer joy had forced Brianna to participate in the business of living, even when she hadn't felt like it.

After her husband had been killed and she'd left the marshals, she'd lived in total isolation. Or she would have, if not for Ruthie. Without her daughter, Brianna had no doubt she would have squirreled her way into a box and never come out but for the occasional trip to the grocery store. Even that could have been avoided with the existence of home delivery.

Ruthie had forced her to open the door, however narrow that opening. She had a tendency to remain aloof, her shoulders rigid, her eyes wary, as she assessed everyone with an eye to them being a possible threat.

That was how she'd stayed alive, but it was no way to live. Gradually, Ruthie's needs and engaging personality had enticed Brianna to find joy in small things.

With each step they'd taken—together—Brianna had found her way back to the land of the living.

None of that had prepared her, though, for seeing Gideon again. He'd been right to try to ease the awkwardness between them. The last time they'd seen each other had been at Rex Jameson's trial.

The vile things the man had hurled at her, at Gideon, at everyone in the courtroom, had burned their way into her brain.

She wanted to feel relieved that she was no longer alone in taking care of Ruthie, but she didn't. She wanted to feel comforted by Gideon's presence, but she didn't. She wanted to feel safe, but she didn't.

At the heart of everything was a fear so huge that she felt as though it could swallow her whole. If she allowed even the smallest chink in the shield she'd built around herself, she feared she would disintegrate. The determination that had gotten her through every day of the last six years would dissolve, and then where would she be? She couldn't afford to rely on anyone but herself. And the Lord.

Not even Gideon.

She shored up her courage and reminded herself that she was responsible for her and Ruthie's safety.

With that resolve, she slid into bed, but she couldn't fall asleep.

How could she?

Grateful that the cabin was big enough that he and Brianna and Ruthie weren't living on top of each other, Gideon had settled in the nook off the kitchen and opened his laptop. Morning sunlight streamed through two high windows, making it a pleasant spot with plenty of light. He still had S&J operations to oversee and wanted to stay on top of things as best he could.

When Shelley Rabb Judd, founder of S&J Security/Protection, had offered him the job of overseeing the Colorado branch of the company, he'd jumped at the opportunity. He both liked and respected his coworkers, men and women Shelley had recruited from the spec op community and law enforcement. Moreover, he liked the work, helping people who felt they had nowhere else to turn.

The small area, which contained a washer and dryer and also served as a mudroom, was private enough that he could work on his laptop.

The cat who was part of the package of Brianna and Ruthie now wound her way between his legs. Gideon bent down to scratch Miso between her ears. Bodyguard to a cat. Who would have thought?

Much to his surprise, Miso was growing on him. He'd never had a pet—not as a child, and certainly not as an adult. There'd been no money as a child for such "foolishness," as his mother had put it when he'd begged for a dog or a cat, and no time as an adult.

"You like Miso, don't you?" Ruthie asked as she joined him at the desk. Without giving him an opportunity to answer, she said, "She likes you, too. Otherwise, she'd just leave you alone. Or she might even hiss at you. She hissed at Mommy once when Mommy was trying to give her a pill." The little girl was silent for a moment, considering. "But Miso didn't mean it. She likes Mommy. Well, most of the time, anyway."

Gideon absorbed the barrage of information about the cat. "Good to know."

"You like Mommy, too." Ruthie's eyes turned knowing.

Caught off guard and struggling to keep up with Ruthie's hopscotching from subject to subject, he finally said, "Yeah. I guess I do."

"She likes you, too. I can tell."

"How do you know?" Gideon felt like a heel pumping a child for information, but he couldn't help himself. "Did she say something?" He winced at that, hoping that he didn't sound desperate.

"No. But I see the way she looks at you. Her eyes get this funny look in them, like she's trying not to like you but she does anyway." Ruthie gave him a frank appraisal. "When you think no one's looking, you look at her like you really like her, too, but don't want her to know."

She could lead seminars for law-enforcement agencies all over the world, giving them tips on reading micro-expressions, those telltale signs that skilled interrogators looked for when questioning a suspect.

"Why don't you want Mommy to know that you like her?" Ruthie asked. "When I like someone, I tell them. It makes them feel good."

Okay. This was getting way too personal. Ruthie was a cute kid, but she unnerved him with her insightful questions and her big eyes that seemed to see everything.

"You should tell Mommy that you like her. It would make her feel good. She tries to hide it when she's sad, but I know that she is sad now." Ruthie fisted tiny hands on tiny hips, looking adorably fierce. "I think you should tell her right now."

"Uh…it's not that easy for grown-ups to say that."

"Why not?"

Why not? "Because grown-ups have a lot of things that can get in the way."

"Like what?"

The conversation was becoming a duel of words, and he was losing to a pint-size master interrogator.

"How about this? I'll tell her when I think the time is right."

Ruthie appeared to consider the proposal. "All right. But don't forget. Sometimes grown-ups forget what they're supposed to do." Her chin inched up, as though she was daring him to break his promise.

"I won't."

She patted his hand. "Don't feel bad. You're doing a good job of taking care of Mommy," the little girl said with childlike frankness. "I'm glad. She's always worrying. I know because she gets little lines right here." Ruthie pointed to the small space between her eyebrows.

"I'm doing my best to take care of both of you."

"And Miso," Ruthie added solemnly.

"And Miso," Gideon said, equally solemnly.

"Mommy says when we do our best, we're doing what Jesus wants us to."

He wasn't ready to get into a theological discussion with a five-year-old, especially when he figured she'd beat him hands down, so he contented himself by taking a different tack. "Your mommy's a smart lady."

Ruthie looked pleased. "I think so, too." She chewed on her bottom lip. "I'm smart, too, but not as smart as Mommy. But someday I will be."

Gideon chuckled. "I think you're pretty smart right now."

"That's what my preschool teacher said." This was said without a hint of false modesty, which made him chuckle again.

"Well, there you go." He searched for something to say that didn't sound like gibberish. Talking down to a child, particularly one as bright as Ruthie, wouldn't win him any points.

He'd held his own defending his actions with ranking officers in the Joint Special Operations Command, but he was struggling to carry on a conversation with a five-year-old. He wouldn't be surprised if even the chiefs of JSOC would have to scramble to keep up with the child across from him.

"I'm glad you're here." The honest words said in a little-girl voice reached down and squeezed his heart.

"Thank you. I'm glad I'm here, too." At this moment in time, there was no place he'd rather be.

"That's good. It's no fun being where you don't want to be."

The words held a profound truth that belied their simplicity. The little girl was not only intelligent, but also perceptive. No wonder he was floundering in his conversation with her.

He could learn a lot from her observations. Like being honest with others even when it was uncomfortable. Could he do that with Brianna? Did he want to?

He didn't know.

Gideon didn't fool himself into believing that it was going to be easy sharing the cabin with Brianna and Ruthie. The extreme cold made it difficult—if not impossible—to spend much time outside. In the summer, he'd have taken them to a favorite picnic spot in a high meadow and spent the day exploring.

He'd had the house stocked not only with food, but also with games for all ages. Maybe they'd get a rousing game of *Candy Land* going. The idea had his lips tipping up at the corners. He didn't have any experience being around young children and had a feeling that he had a lot to learn, but he'd picked up on one thing already. Don't talk down to them.

In the meantime, maybe he could win some points by whipping up a breakfast to tempt a five-year-old.

Gideon would be the first to admit that he wasn't much of a cook, but he prided himself on his pancakes, which, he'd been told by the few friends he had entertained in his condo, were light and fluffy.

"How about I fix you a pancake?" he said.

"Can you make it look like a cat?" Ruthie asked.

He went to work, and after a few minutes of prep, with a few deft twists of a spoon and spatula, he shaped the batter into a cat. After flipping it, he presented the plate to Ruthie with a flourish.

She stared at the cat-shaped pancake. "What's that?"

"What do you mean, 'what's that?' It's a cat. Like Miso."

Ruthie turned a disbelieving look on him. "It doesn't look anything like a cat. It looks like a mouse. A mouse with a really big head."

Gideon drew himself up in mock umbrage. "It's the best-looking cat I've ever seen. Except for Miso. Maybe we should ask her about it."

Ruthie giggled. "That's silly. Miso can't talk."

"She can recognize one of her own kind."

"I'll get her." The little girl retreated from the room, then returned carrying a displeased-looking Miso. "Tell Gideon that it doesn't look like a cat," Ruthie told her pet.

Miso gave a sniff, jumped down from Ruthie's arms and stalked off, tail held regally in the air.

His sense of humor kicked in at the scenario.

He had been a highly trained and decorated Navy SEAL and a US Marshal, and he had effectively been put in his place by a small child and a know-it-all cat.

The cat pancake seemed to look less like a cat with every second. The more he looked at it, the more it started looking like a mouse. Maybe Ruthie had a point. "Why don't you try the pancake, anyway?"

Ruthie cut a small piece and popped it into her mouth. "It's pretty good. Even if it doesn't look like a cat." She ate the entire pancake and held out her plate. "Can you make a dog this time?"

"Maybe I should just stick with round ones," he said humbly.

She nodded with a judicious air. "You're probably right. Round pancakes taste almost as good as cat or dog ones. Plus, they're easier to make. You know, for people like you who aren't very good at making them." She added the last with a sympathetic look.

"Good to know."

The conversation was a ridiculous one, but he was enjoying it more than he'd enjoyed anything in a long time.

He whipped up another pancake, cooked it and flipped it onto her plate. "Here you go."

She turned her attention to the second pancake, finishing it off in short order. "Thank you for breakfast," she said politely and took off, calling Miso as she ran out of the kitchen.

He heard a soft chuckle and turned to find Brianna smiling at him. "Looks like you're gonna have to up your pancake game."

He assumed a mock-fierce persona once more. "Who says?"

"Ruthie and Miso."

"You're right. Do you want to try a pancake? I've got more batter."

Her brow lifted. "Will it be shaped like a cat?"

He let his shoulders droop. "I'm afraid not. I have it on good authority that my cat pancakes aren't all that good."

Brianna's smile broadened. "Don't let it get to you. Ruthie can be a tough customer." Her teasing abruptly vanished, and her gaze turned somber. "Thank you for being so good with her. Things haven't been easy for her. Especially now. She was just getting settled after our last move, even making a friend. She's never had a real friend before."

"Things couldn't have been easy for you, either," he said gently, thinking of what she'd been through in the last six years.

She made a face. "I'm a mom. They're not supposed to be easy for me."

"It must be hard, raising her on your own."

"We make do."

"Do you ever want…more?" He held his breath as he waited. She wouldn't know how important her answer was to him. Honesty forced him to silently acknowledge that he wanted a life with Brianna and Ruthie, a family like the kind he'd never had.

He had no clue as to what Brianna would think. Would she be willing to risk her and Ruthie's happiness on a loner like him, a man who had all but shunned the company of others?

What did he know about being a father? With so few years with his real dad, he had only the brutal example of his stepfather.

"More?"

"Forget it." What was he thinking? Brianna had enough facing her without him burdening her with his feelings. He turned his back to her as he busied himself at the stove. "One pancake coming up." In a minute, he slid the pancake onto a plate and set it in front of her.

She seemed as relieved as he was to drop the subject. "Thanks," she said as he slid the syrup and butter her way.

He made one for himself, and they busied themselves with the meal, but a part of him couldn't help wishing they could have finished the conversation.

In the great room, Brianna watched as Ruthie played "house" with the cat, herself as the mommy and Miso as the little girl. At times, she praised Miso, but she also scolded her.

Was that how she sounded? Brianna wondered. Alternating between praising and scolding? She hoped she did more of the former, but she couldn't be certain. She knew she was extra strict with safety precautions, but she had reasons.

Now she questioned if she'd been too strict, if she'd denied Ruthie simple childhood pleasures by always insisting on keeping to themselves. Only in the last year had she loosened the reins, and then, only a small amount.

Now she gazed lovingly at her daughter, the best thing to have ever happened to her. Perhaps the only thing she'd done right. No, that wasn't true. She'd been a good marshal. Once. She'd tried to be a good wife. She'd failed at that, but she'd tried. Oh, how she'd tried.

Though Jack hadn't been a believer, she'd asked him to join her in prayer. He'd grudgingly accepted a few times, then turned her invitations away. Eventually, he'd started to openly mock her beliefs until she'd kept her prayers private.

Not for the first time, she asked herself what had happened to him, what had happened to them. It had been more than Jack's contempt for her belief, though, that had put a wedge between them. He had started mocking everything about her, including her work as a marshal.

Without her being aware of it, Ruthie came to stand at her side. "Mommy, you look sad."

With a determined effort, Brianna wiped the melancholy from her eyes and worked up a smile. "No sad going on here. The cabin is a happy place."

"Good. Because Miso and I want to play with you."

"Did Miso tell you that?"

Ruthie leaned in closer. "She meowed it."

Brianna assumed an appropriately impressed expression. "Miso is very smart."

"That's what Gideon said."

"I think Gideon's pretty smart, too."

"He's pretty smart," Ruthie agreed. "But not as smart as you or Miso."

Flattered that she'd received top billing in the smart department, Brianna smiled. "Thank you."

"You're the best mommy ever."

Tears stung her eyes. "Thank you, sweetheart. And you're the best daughter in the whole world." She hugged Ruthie and decided things weren't so bad, not as long as she had this precious child in her life.

For the space that it took one heartbeat to give way to the next, she knew a strange, almost improper contentment in being in the cabin with Ruthie and Miso.

And Gideon.

Her feelings for him were growing, and though she tried to tell herself that they were born out of gratitude for his keeping her and Ruthie safe, she knew they were much more complex.

"You like Gideon, don't you?" Ruthie asked.

How did she explain her feelings for him to her daughter when couldn't even explain them to herself?

"I guess I do."

Ruthie nodded, as though Brianna had confirmed what she already knew. "That's good. So do I."

Brianna smiled, but her thoughts were still wrapped up in understanding what was happening to her. It was as though she was balanced on a thin strip of happiness high above a dangerous chasm. One wrong step, one false move, and she feared she would take a deadly tumble.

She couldn't afford a misstep, not when her and Ruthie's lives depended upon her ability to keep them safe.

If it had been only her own life, things would have been different, but Ruthie's life was precious beyond measure.

Rex Jameson's words whispered through her memory, and a shudder rippled through her as she recalled every hate-filled word spewing from his mouth at the end of the trial, turning the air in the courtroom putrid with his filth. She doubted anyone who had been there that day had forgotten the ugly threats he'd issued.

The words were seared into her brain: *I'll show up when you least expect it. And what I'll do to you won't be nice and neat like the bullet your man took. Think on that.*

Even in prison, he'd held a chilling power over her, his words filling her with the need to scan every doorway, every window she passed, wondering if some ominous silhouette would pop out at her.

Her life had become a frightening landscape where shadows lurked everywhere.

To reassure herself, she bent down and wrapped her arms around Ruthie, causing her daughter to pull back and give her a questioning look.

"Are you all right, Mommy?"

"I'm fine." Brianna released Ruthie, at the same time trying to force Jameson's threats from her mind.

A shiver raced through her before she squelched it. Jameson was relentless. She straightened her shoulders. He'd find that she could be just as relentless.

SEVEN

Gideon wandered into the great room and observed the hug between mother and daughter, more moved than he'd expected. He'd never been around small children, any children for that matter, and hadn't known what to expect.

The unabashed love Brianna and her daughter shared touched him in the soft places that he'd believed war and tracking down felons in the marshals service had totally erased. He'd seen too much, done too much, to view the world with anything but cynical eyes, but what he'd just witnessed had tempered that cynicism, if only by a bit.

This was only temporary, he reminded himself. He wasn't part of this family, and he'd do well to keep that in mind.

The self-directed reminder in place, he was free to watch mother and daughter, and enjoy the picture they made. There was little of Jack in the young girl's features except for the jut of her small chin—the one that said she was her own person and woe to anyone who tried to say different. Otherwise, she was all Brianna, but in miniature.

His own family, long since gone, had never indulged in the kind of play he saw now. There was only work and more work. Between his step-father's rages that often resulted in beatings and his mother's apathy, there was little else but the drudgery of two jobs apiece and the constant struggle to put food on the table and make rent.

He'd turned out all right. Rather than going to college after high school, as most of his friends had, he'd enlisted in the navy. From there, he'd set his sights on the SEALs. The rigorous program had honed his determination to make something of himself.

Making it through BUD/S had forced him to take stock of himself. He was the first to admit that he'd slacked off in high school, nearly hadn't graduated. He hadn't seen his life as anything more than a series of dead-end jobs. The navy had changed that. The SEALs had changed it yet again.

Being a part of those elite warriors who were often called the tip of the spear in America's war on terror had given him the direction he'd been seeking without being aware of it. From there, the move to the US Marshals seemed a natural transition.

After his partner's death, he knew he could no longer stay with the marshals. Taking the job with S&J Security/Protection had been a no-brainer. He'd been fortunate to land with a firm that cared about people more than the bottom line.

He set his laptop on a small desk and straddled a chair, needing to check in with operatives handling other cases.

Ruthie perched on a stool beside Gideon and peered intently at the screen. He quickly blanked it and turned to smile at her.

"Do you want to play with Miso and me?" Ruthie asked.

"Uh…" What did he know about playing with a little girl and her cat?

"Ruthie, what did I tell you about bothering Gideon?" Brianna's voice saved him from having to come up with a response.

Ruthie aimed her too-perceptive gaze at him. "I'm not bothering you, am I?"

"No, you're not." He looked at Brianna. "We're getting along fine."

She sent a disapproving look at her daughter. "Still, she knows better than to disturb you when you're working."

Gideon gave a wry smile. "I wish I was getting something done."

"Maybe if you have some quiet, you would."

Ruthie bent to pick up Miso. "Miso and I'll go in the other room."

"You're not bothering—" He stopped. Ruthie and Miso were already walking out of the room. Her little shoulders drooped, whether under the weight of carrying Miso or from her mother's chastisement, Gideon wasn't certain.

"Sorry about that," Brianna said.

"There's nothing to apologize for. She's a cute kid. And smart, too."

"Too smart, sometimes. She keeps me on my toes. The questions she asks would stump a *Jeopardy* contestant."

"She'd keep an entire SEAL team on its toes."

Brianna grinned. "Trying to keep up with her is a full-time job, believe me."

"Oh, I do."

"Sometimes I wonder what Jack would think of her." The humor had left Brianna's voice. In its place was a sad contemplation, as though she was afraid she knew the answer but didn't want to acknowledge it. Why would she question what her husband would have thought of their child?

"He'd be proud of her," Gideon said quietly.

"Would he? I don't know. At one time, I thought I did. I thought I knew everything about him and that he felt the same about me. That ended not long into our marriage."

He didn't know what to say. He'd thought that Brianna, or Leah as she was then, and Jack had a strong marriage and a good life together. Should he ask her if she wanted to talk about it? Finally, he said, "Any father would be proud of Ruthie and how you've raised her."

"Thank you. You always did know the right thing to say. That's one of the things I missed about you." Something flashed in her eyes, something he wished he knew how to interpret.

"You missed me?" He wanted to pull back the words. What was he thinking? He forced out a laugh. "That came out wrong. Sorry."

"Don't be. I missed you. A lot."

And I missed you. But he didn't say it aloud. The conversation was getting too personal. And personal was something they couldn't afford. Not now. Not when he was supposed to be protecting Brianna and Ruthie from harm.

"Your friendship was one of the best things about being a marshal," Brianna added.

His friendship. He got it. And berated himself for thinking there could be anything else between them. With a sharp reminder to himself that he was there to protect her, and nothing else, he gave a nod that he hoped came off as casual. "Thanks. The same for me." Had he struck the right chord?

Right about now, he was wishing that Ruthie

was with them. Being alone with Brianna was
awkward in the extreme. She must have felt so
as well, for she shifted back and forth on her feet
until he wondered if she'd wear out the soles of
her shoes.

There was so much he wanted to say, so much
he wanted to ask, and because it was all so important, more than he wanted to admit, he said
nothing. How did he tell her what had been in
his heart for the last six years? He couldn't. Especially when he had no idea of her feelings.
And when guilt colored everything he thought
and felt about her.

That wasn't true, he reminded himself. She'd
just told him what she wanted from him. Friendship.

The silence stretched taut between them, and
he nearly jumped when she spoke. "We can't hide
out here forever."

"No." But a small part of him wished that they
could. These few days of being with Brianna and
Ruthie and, yes, Miso, were among the most satisfying he could remember in a long time. With
a start, he realized he'd been lonely, and not just
for people, but for the right people. Family.

Brianna and Ruthie felt like family.

The admission startled him. And scared him
more than a little.

What did he know about them, anyway? And

what did he know about families? He'd never had a real one.

Until this moment, he hadn't acknowledged the vague feeling that something was missing in his life.

Immediately he rejected the idea. His life was exactly what he wanted. What he'd chosen. He was head of S&J's Colorado operations. He had colleagues he both admired and respected, and work that was satisfying.

He forced his mind back to that work, and the reason Nate had brought him in on this. Rex Jameson.

Six years ago, Gideon and his partner had been tasked with bringing in Jameson when he'd escaped from federal custody.

Jameson had been on his way to ADX Florence, located in the foothills of the Colorado Rockies. Also known as a supermax, the prison was designed to incarcerate and isolate those criminals deemed too violent and dangerous for the average prison system.

Its reputation had earned it the nickname "Alcatraz of the Rockies." Once there, prisoners spent twenty-three hours a day in their cells. Few prisoners ever walked out. Unless, like Jameson, a mistake was found in the original trial.

Gideon had enlisted the help of the Colorado S&J office, asking that operatives keep their ears to the ground in the event that they might hear something and to check in with their CIs. Confidential informants picked up a lot of information that others were not privy to.

No sightings on Jameson. Nothing. It was as though he had disappeared. Even though he was free to come and go as he pleased, he'd stayed under the radar.

Gideon didn't deceive himself into believing the danger was over. On the contrary, he was more apprehensive than ever. Jameson was out there unrestricted and was beyond dangerous.

Releasing him had set in motion a chain of events that Gideon feared would continue. How many more murders would there be until Rex Jameson was captured or killed?

And why now?

He couldn't shake the question.

Why did it take six years for the chain-of-evidence error to be detected?

That question taunted him, worming its way into his thoughts.

As Gideon chewed on that, he wondered if he and Nate had it backward. Could Jameson be the puppet rather than the puppet master? He'd committed at least three murders, including Jack's, and probably more that the authorities hadn't been able to pin on him. In addition, he had staged six bank robberies, but was he only a front man while someone else was directing the action from behind the scenes?

If so, who?

Who had the most to gain with Jameson's release from prison? "Follow the money" was a cliché for a reason. It was true, not just in corporate America, but in organized crime. Mob leaders needed money to operate, just as CEOs did.

Gideon continued to ponder Jameson's unexpected release. It had come about so swiftly that he had not really considered all the workings it had taken to make it possible. Supposedly, Jameson's lawyer had discovered the chain-of-custody error and had brought it to the attention of the court.

But *how* had he discovered it? Had he been reviewing the case and following up on any loose ends when he'd run across it? Or did he receive a tip to look at that point specifically? And, if so, who had given it to him? Could someone in the lab's office have passed it along? That didn't seem likely.

What if the tip had been anonymous? The implications of that were chilling. It meant someone else wanted Jameson out of jail.

As far as Gideon knew, Jameson had no close family, no one who would miss him. He took pride in being a loner. Those who took orders from him feared him, knowing that crossing him would mean certain death.

Within two months of Jameson's release, three people had been murdered. It stood to reason that Jameson was behind the killings, but could that logic be faulty? What if someone else was killing off the people on Jameson's hit list and letting him take the blame?

But to what purpose?

Who else would have reason to get rid of the judge and two witnesses involved in the trial? With each question came more questions, until Gideon had a string of them. The only thing they had in common was the fact that he had answers to none of them.

Who stood to benefit with Jameson on the outside? Gideon thought through the possible ramifications. Perhaps a better question was, who stood to lose with him on the inside?

They were stockpiling until his brain felt overwhelmed and overworked, like an airport trying to juggle dozens of flights without sufficient runways.

He had no doubt that he could find the answers. Eventually. But could he find them in time to save Brianna and Ruthie?

And himself?

"Jameson's going to find us sooner or later," Gideon said. "It's not *if* he finds us. It's *when*."

The afternoon was quiet as he and Brianna sat

across from each other at the table. With Ruthie taking a nap, they could talk without interruption. The winter sun slanted through the window's wooden blinds, casting bars of light on the table's surface.

The cabin felt safe and snug, tucked away where no one could find them. At least, that was how Brianna wanted to think of it, but Gideon was right.

Jameson had unlimited resources and contacts. If he wanted to find them, he would.

"I know."

"We need to be prepared. That means having go-bags ready."

"Ruthie and I always have our bags packed," Brianna reminded him quietly. "It's how we've had to live."

She and Ruthie had lived with the ever-present knowledge that they would have to uproot their lives at a moment's notice.

"How many times have you moved?" he asked.

"Five. It wasn't that there was always a threat, but it seemed wise to not stay in one place for too long." Jameson had kept her hostage with his threats as effectively as if he'd imprisoned her. But instead of sitting behind bars, she was running. Always running.

"We couldn't take much with us, so we shopped at flea markets for furniture and stuff each time we moved to a new place. That's how we found Miso. We heard a noise coming from a dresser drawer. When we pulled it open, there was this tiny kitten tucked inside. We asked around, but no one claimed her, so we took her home with us."

"Sounds like a hard way to live."

She shook her head at the pity she read in his gaze. Pity was the last thing she wanted.

"Don't feel sorry for us," she said. "We've made a good life for ourselves. We just know not to get too attached to any one place."

"You're pretty amazing," he said.

"Ruthie and I do what we have to."

"You make a pretty good team."

"Well, we're not quite at the level of your SEAL team, but we do okay." Her throat felt scratchy, as though tiny thorns coated it, turning her voice husky. She cleared it with an abrupt cough, and hoped Gideon hadn't noticed the emotion that threatened to spill out.

"You do more than okay," he said in a low voice.

"I know this—" she spread her arms to encompass the cabin "—is only temporary. But it feels like home."

The concern in his eyes reminded her that they weren't there for an idyllic winter vacation, but to escape a killer.

"When it comes time for a showdown, don't count me out. Remember, it's not the size of the dog in the fight, it's the—"

"The size of the fight in the dog," he said, finishing for her.

She smiled, recalling she'd quoted the idiom to him more than once when they'd served together in the marshals.

"I may have lost a step or two, but I can still hold my own."

"I never doubted it. You were one of the best—at driving, shooting and close-quarters combat."

Her smile broadened. She'd taken him down more than once in training sessions of CQC.

"But you still don't think I can cut it if we're ever under attack."

He didn't sugarcoat his words. "I think you'll be busy protecting Ruthie," he said. "You may not be able to do both."

Her eyes narrowed in a wince as she acknowledged that he was right. She wanted to promise that she'd always have his back, but she couldn't.

If it came to taking out an enemy or safeguarding her child, she wouldn't have a choice. She wouldn't have a choice at all.

Gideon saw the distress in her expression. "Don't beat yourself up over it. That's the way it should be. A mother takes care of her child."

The way his mother hadn't taken care of him. She'd done her best, he supposed, but she'd never been able to stand up to his stepfather, a man who used a belt and fists to make his point. When Gideon had tried to protect his mother from his stepfather's wrath on one occasion, he'd been beaten unconscious and then locked in a closet for twenty-four hours.

When he went silent for a long minute, Brianna leaned forward, concern in her eyes. "What is it? What's hurting you?"

"Nothing."

"You're a good man, Gideon. Jack always said so."

"Jack was one of the best agents I've ever worked with." He paused. "I'm sorry. I didn't mean to stir up memories."

"You didn't," she said, but a sadness had crept into her voice even as sorrow worked its way into her eyes. "It's okay. I lost Jack a long time before he died."

He tilted his head in an invitation for her to continue as seconds stretched into minutes. He wondered if she regretted going there.

"Jack was a good marshal. He was good at everything he did." She smiled sadly. "Everything except for being a husband."

Gideon didn't say anything, only nodded to show that he was listening.

Brianna bowed her head in her hands, then raised it and pushed her hair back from her face. "You may not want to hear this."

"I think I need to hear it," he answered. What could she tell him about Jack that he didn't already know? The two men had been partners for three years. There was little they hadn't talked about on the long protective details they'd spent together.

Gideon had shared the details of his childhood, something he'd never talked about with anyone until then.

Jack hadn't tried to talk him out of his feelings, had only gripped Gideon's shoulder and listened without judging.

In turn, Gideon had listened while Jack shared his dream of moving up in the marshals. He'd been ambitious and wanted to go all the way.

"Jack was very competitive. You know that. He was determined to be the best. Not just the best, but the best of the best." At Gideon's nod, she said, "At the same time, I was rising fast in the service. Faster than Jack, as good as he was. He didn't like it. That may be the biggest understatement of all time." She laughed, but there was no humor in the sound, only a hollow ring.

"At work, he was all supportive and pretended to be proud of me, but when we were at home, he let me know that the only reason I was promoted before him was that I was a woman and the service was trying to meet federal quotas. For a while I wondered if he could be right and started doubting myself. It took a toll on my work, and I started making mistakes."

She shook her head. "Maybe I was letting the promotions go to my head. I didn't think so, but by the end he had me doubting everything I did, everything I said. I was terrified I was going to make an unforgivable mistake, something that would cost a witness or a colleague his or her life."

"You know better than that. You were one of the best." Jack had caused her to doubt her abilities and, worse, herself.

"Jack didn't see it that way. Once I won a shooting competition. He sulked about it for days, even demanded that the scores be recounted. By the end, I was so embarrassed that I wished I'd never entered the contest.

"I won't say that it didn't hurt," Brianna continued. "Because it did. I worked hard. Harder than any man, but I did my best to downplay any special assignments I was given. It didn't help. When I didn't tell him that I'd received a commendation—an in-office, no-big-deal one—he accused me of patronizing him, which made him angrier than ever. Nothing I could do was right.

"Finally, I was ready to call it quits."

"You mean leave him?"

She shook her head. "Leave the service. When Jack and I married, I took vows, and I meant them."

"You'd have left the marshals?"

She'd loved her job, and she was good at it. It angered him that she'd even considered quitting. And though she'd left the job in the end, that was for a different reason.

"Without the job, I thought maybe we could put our marriage back together." She gave another of those hollow laughs. "I knew it was unlikely we could mend what was broken, but at that point, I was willing to try anything. I was making plans to resign just before Jack died.

"We had a fight that night." She closed her eyes to block out the memory. "It was a bad one. We said hideous things to each other. When I learned he'd been killed, I wondered…"

"You wondered if he'd been distracted."

Her nod was jerky. "I couldn't help it. A month after his death, I found out that I was expecting. I'd wanted a baby for a long time, but Jack always had an excuse why we couldn't start a family, and by that time, things were so bad between us that I'd stopped wishing for a child.

"It was this wonderful blessing that I'd never dreamed would be mine."

Gideon smiled. "You're a great mother."

"I have a great kid."

"Still, it couldn't have been easy, raising Ruthie on your own and trying to stay under the radar at the same time."

"No, it wasn't. But I wouldn't take back one minute of it. Ruthie gives me a reason to get up every morning."

"I wish I'd known. About Jack, I mean. Maybe I could have done something. Talked to him. Something."

"There's nothing you could have done. Jack's ego was threatened. He couldn't stand the idea that his wife might be better than him at something."

A flush crept up her cheeks. "I'm talking too much. Put it down to stress. Jack did his best, and he was a good marshal."

But Gideon wondered.

Gideon looked like he wanted to say something more, but he didn't, and Brianna was grateful that he had let the matter drop, intuitively knowing that delving too deeply would complicate things between them. Talking about that time in her life wasn't easy, and she wondered why she'd shared as much as she had with him. Maybe it was because Gideon had always been easy to talk to.

Unlike Jack, he had applauded her rise in the

marshals and been genuinely happy for any success she'd achieved. Remembered warmth filled her as she recalled his quiet words of praise when she'd been awarded a commendation of valor.

She turned the subject to him. "What made you decide to leave the marshals service?"

He gave her a you-ought-to-know look. "With everything that went down, I couldn't stay any longer. I put out some feelers and ended up with S and J. I heard about the firm overseas, learned that they hired spec ops and ex–law enforcement. I decided to give it a try. It's been good so far. What about you? How did you get by these last years?"

"I found an analyst job for a small corporation. Turns out they were glad to let me work from home. When I had to leave, I found another analyst job. It made things easier when Ruthie was born."

"She looks just like you. Not much like Jack at all. Except maybe around the eyes."

She smiled at that but didn't comment. "We couldn't risk making friends, until Ruthie started preschool and found a little girl she liked, but we've been doing okay on our own. Until…"

"Until Jameson was set free."

She let a nod answer for her.

"It sounds like a lonely life."

"It was. But we had each other. We were getting by. But now…"

He reached for her hand, gave it a quick squeeze. "We'll get Jameson and put him back where he belongs."

"I just don't get it. If he's on the run, why is he taking the time to come after me?" She heard the quaver in her voice and flushed at the foolishness of it.

Gideon didn't answer right away. After a few beats, he said, "You know who he is. What he is. His hatred is like a festering wound."

Her eyebrows drew together, and she nodded in one resigned motion. "You're right. Revenge matters more to him than his freedom." Fear overcame her as she added, "If he ever got his hands on Ruthie—"

She didn't have to finish, knowing that Gideon understood. Jameson would use Ruthie against her. He wouldn't care that she was only a little girl.

"We won't let him near her," Gideon promised.

"I just so wanted to believe that he'd forgotten about me."

"Jameson won't stop until somebody stops him. He isn't capable of backing down."

"I remember," Brianna said quietly, "though I did my best to forget."

"I won't lie to you. It's going to take everything we have to stay one step ahead of him."

A festering wound.

The words stuck in Brianna's mind. Gideon was right. Jameson wasn't going to forget his vow of revenge.

He wasn't capable of forgetting…or forgiving.

EIGHT

When the burner phone he'd purchased chirped, Gideon tensed. He hadn't expected to use it. The only person he'd given the number to was Nate, who had emphasized avoiding using it unless it was a true emergency.

His friend didn't bother with greetings. "We need to meet. There's something you need to know. Something I can't tell you over the phone."

The strain in Nate's voice caused Gideon to move out of Brianna's earshot. Nate didn't sound like himself. Normally he took everything thrown at him in stride. But now there was alarm and urgency in his tone.

"Okay. When and where?"

"Do you remember where we went fishing two summers ago?"

Gideon got it. Nate didn't want to give voice to the location, even on what was supposed to be a secure line.

"Yeah." They'd gone fishing at a secluded lake,

staying in a cabin that had belonged to Nate's uncle. They had come away from the trip with a cooler full of trout and enough tall fish stories to last a lifetime. Gideon smiled at the memory.

"There. The south side. Eight." The terseness of Nate's answer wiped away Gideon's smile. "Watch out for tails."

"And you watch your six."

A low chuckle. "You better know it."

Gideon disconnected and walked back into the kitchen, where Brianna was waiting, an expectant expression in her eyes.

"Who was that?"

"Nate. He wants to meet."

Surprise registered in her eyes. "I thought he wanted us to stay off the grid."

"He did. Whatever this is must be important. Important enough to break protocol."

"I don't like the idea of you going alone."

"And I don't like leaving you and Ruthie here alone."

They couldn't take Ruthie with them. And truth be told, he didn't want Brianna along, either. Whatever Nate had to tell him sounded serious enough to cause Gideon to take extra precautions.

After making certain that the cabin was locked up tight and that Brianna had her weapon on her, he felt ready to leave. He had an errand to do before meeting Nate.

Despite the safeguards he took, though, he still feared leaving Brianna and Ruthie unprotected.

"I can take care of us," she said, apparently guessing his thoughts.

"I know."

He stepped toward the door, but she tugged his arm. "Be careful, Gideon." The words were whispered, adding to their poignancy.

He took her concern with him out into the cold bluster of the wind.

An hour later, he drove away from a used-car lot in a beat-up pickup truck. A blizzard was approaching, and he wanted something more substantial than the minivan to navigate treacherous mountain roads. The battered truck wasn't much to look at, but it boasted heavy-duty tires and a rugged suspension system.

He then made the thirty-minute drive to the lake where he and Nate had spent a long-ago summer.

It was dusk when he arrived, the time of evening that was neither day nor night. Gideon had never liked the twilight hour that cast everything in shadow and made it difficult to identify the presence of danger.

The air was cold enough that he could see his own breath, little clouds of it that would give him away to anyone watching, and he cupped his hand over his mouth to shield it. Giving away a position could be deadly. He'd learned that lesson the hard way while in the SEALs, when one of his teammates had let down his guard. The man—a friend, a brother—had died instantly from a double tap to the forehead.

He didn't have to wait for Nate. His friend was already there and motioned to his car. Nate slid in the driver's side while Gideon climbed in the passenger side.

The two men fist-bumped.

"You weren't followed?" Nate made a question out of the words.

"What do you think?"

"Good. Sorry about all the cloak-and-dagger, but this thing has me looking over my shoulder more than usual."

"What's going on?"

Nate peered through the windshield, as though trying to find answers in the darkness. "You heard about the software that we use in placing witnesses. We were just getting it started around the time you left."

"I heard rumors about it back then. Supposed to be the biggest thing since sliced bread."

"It totally revolutionized the WITSEC system. We were able to keep track of our people in real time."

Gideon nodded. Time was essential in protecting witnesses. If a threat was made, getting to the people immediately could make the difference between life and death. It wasn't just the lives of the witnesses at stake. Family members were often involved, as many agreeing to go into the WITSEC program wouldn't do so without their families.

Nate's expression was tight and drawn.

Gideon felt his stomach muscles clench.

"There's something you need to know." Nate's voice was low, urgent. "Something's going on with WITSEC. We've lost three witnesses in the last two months. As far as I know, the people have been following the rules, not drawing attention to themselves, showing up for work—you know the drill."

"Were their families executed as well?"

Nate's nod was grim. "Two were single, but the others were married. In all four cases, the spouses were killed, too." His mouth twisted. "If there's a bright spot in this whole debacle, it's that the children—five, altogether—were spared." He laughed, but there was no humor in it. "What do you know? A killer with a conscience."

Gideon understood the need to find any kind of bright spot to hold on to. If those who worked in law enforcement didn't, if they allowed the horrors they witnessed on a regular basis to get to them, they wouldn't last long. Not professionally, not emotionally.

"There's more."

"Tell me."

"The leaks are coming from our office. One of our own is betraying us."

That troubled Gideon almost as much as the deaths, as he knew most of the people in the Denver office. The idea that one of his former coworkers could betray everything the marshals stood for was abhorrent.

"What are the Feds doing?"

Nate scrubbed his face with his hands. When he pulled his hands away, his eyes were bloodshot.

"What you'd expect. Interviewing everyone who had access to the software. You know the security protocols we have in place. We're upgrading them even as we speak. No one gets clearance until their lives have been turned inside out." He shook his head, overwhelming frustration evident in the single gesture. "Still, names are getting out. Several people have resigned over it. I guess they figured better to resign than get fired. A few at the top level have been fired."

No government agency—or any organization for that matter—was free of human error, but this appeared to have gone far beyond that. If the bad guys got their hands on the software containing the list of witnesses and their new names and locations, it would send every law-enforcement bureau in the country scrambling to scoop up those people and relocate them before they were executed. And now it appeared even that wouldn't be enough.

"Who's heading up this op?" Gideon asked.

"Callahan," Nate replied.

"She's one of the best," Gideon said. "Nothing gets by her." Toria Callahan wasn't one to tolerate fools and had earned the reputation of having an iron fist in a velvet glove.

"Well, something did. Or *someone*," Nate added ominously.

"How do you know the mole's in the Colorado office?"

"I planted some information. Totally bogus, of course, but believable. Two days later, that information was on the dark web. For sale. If it had been legit, it would have earned the seller more money than you or I'll see in our lifetimes.

"It's more than a single person. I'm talking a network. Bigger than I ever imagined." The intensity of his words caused Gideon to lean forward. "It's not just that the mole is selling identities and location, he's also selling the software itself."

Gideon gave a low whistle. Selling the proprietary software developed solely for the US Marshals would compromise not only witnesses in Rex Jameson's case but thousands of other witnesses and their families. No one would be safe.

"Do you know who?"

Nate shook his head. "Not yet. But I'm getting close. I encrypted some fail-safes in the software. If they're tripped, I'll know about it. Digital fingerprints can be hidden, but they can't be erased."

"Does anyone else know what you did?"

"No." Nate frowned. "At least, I don't think so. I haven't told anyone but you about my suspicions. I did everything I could to stay under the radar on this."

It was Gideon's turn to frown now. "You're putting yourself in the line of fire. You know that."

"Can't be helped. When I get more, I'll let you know. Watch your back. Don't trust anyone.

"In the meantime, keep our girl safe. She's not in WITSEC, but she's one of ours. I always wondered if you and she…" Another face scrub. "Never mind."

"I'll keep her safe." The two men reached out to clasp hands.

Right as a gunshot pierced the night.

The shot was accompanied by a hiss of air, the unmistakable sound of a high-powered rifle. The bullet found its mark, drilling a neat hole in Nate's chest.

"Nate! Hold on, buddy," Gideon rasped. "We're getting out of here. Get you help."

Nate shook his head, the effort clearly costing him. "We've been brothers too long for you to lie to me."

Blood spilled from his mouth down his neck. A gurgling sound, frequently described as a death rattle, issued from his chest.

"Hold on," Gideon pleaded. "Hold on." *Don't let him die.* The prayer he hadn't uttered in too long to remember never made it to his lips. Nate let out one last gasp and then went limp.

"No!"

Gideon pulled his hands away from his friend, let them hang uselessly at his sides.

The shooter had hit the wrong target. Given the time of day and the shadowy light through the snow that had begun to fall, the error was not surprising. Just a few inches to the right and the bullet would have killed him, not Nate.

He'd lost other friends, brothers, in the SEALs. You didn't serve in spec ops without losing someone close to you. But losing Nate nearly brought him to his knees.

Nate had a pretty wife and two little boys, with another child on the way. Where was the justice in taking him? Where was the humanity in that?

There was none.

The Lord Gideon had once believed in would

not have allowed such a thing to happen. It only confirmed that he'd been right in turning his back on those beliefs. They had ceased being relevant in his life long ago.

Agony over Nate's death pierced his heart so keenly that he wondered if he had taken a bullet as well. The rumble of an engine turning over reminded him that the shooter was still out there.

So caught up in grief was he over his friend, he hadn't been thinking clearly.

Lives were lost that way.

The sound of that revving engine roared through the night.

Gideon wanted to follow, but it was already too late. Right now there was only one thing to do. Get back to Brianna and Ruthie.

The storm was intensifying, dropping pellets of snow and ice. He had to make it back to the cabin before the roads were closed.

He grabbed Nate's phone, called S&J and filled in his second-in-command about what happened. He then asked the man to call both the police and the marshals' office, and gave the location.

Protocol dictated that he should stay and answer questions, but he immediately rejected the idea. He couldn't leave Brianna alone one more minute than necessary.

He looked at his friend once more. "I won't

stop until I find out who did this to you." With that vow, he got in the truck and sped away.

Brianna didn't need for Gideon to say anything to know that things had gone horribly wrong. It was there on his face. Whatever had happened had been bad. Really, really bad.

The back of her mouth went dry as she braced herself for what he would tell her.

At first glance, he seemed to be carrying himself with his usual vigor, but when she looked more closely, she saw the small dip to his shoulders, as though he didn't have the strength to keep them square and straight.

She didn't pepper him with questions but waited for him to speak. His lips folded in on themselves as if they couldn't get out the words. "Nate's dead," he said after a long moment had passed.

The two words cost him, she saw, and he was silent for a long moment. "A sniper shot. Meant for me. Got Nate instead." Another long pause. "My fault."

She didn't contradict him, didn't rush to fill the void with words of reassurance. He would come to his own conclusions when he wasn't bowed down with grief. She had a dozen questions that the clipped words didn't answer, but she held them back.

He looked up, his eyes dry, as though any tears that might have found their way there couldn't handle the barren plain of his grief.

"I'm sorry," she said, speaking for the first time. "I know he was a friend."

"He was more than a friend. He was my brother." There was the pain. Unspeakable pain, if she was to guess. His shoulders now slumped under the weight of it.

Brianna laid a hand on his shoulder. Gideon had yet to shed a tear, but tears were so thick in her own throat that she couldn't speak.

He stumbled, but when she reached out to steady him, he shook off her hand.

"Don't. Just…don't."

It moved her unbearably to see this strong man break.

"Nate shouldn't have died this way." His voice cracked.

"What can I do?"

He looked up, his gaze so bleak that she willed herself not to look away. He needed her strength, not her sympathy, and she braced herself to do whatever he asked.

Just when she thought he'd sunk into a pit of despair, he rallied. "Be ready to leave when I give the word. Whoever is after us is close. Too close."

It wasn't so much his words as his tone that caused a spasm of fear to shiver down her spine.

* * *

Brianna spent the morning cleaning the already clean cabin, making certain her and Ruthie's belongings were freshly laundered and stowed in their go-bags, and then played hide-and-seek with her daughter.

The game kept Ruthie occupied and forestalled questions she might have asked about Gideon and why he had disappeared into his room without even saying hi to her and Miso.

Brianna had plenty of questions, too—questions like what were they going to do now—but she kept them to herself.

Ruthie's curiosity couldn't be contained forever, though. "Is Gideon sick?"

"He's not feeling well right now," Brianna said in all honesty.

"I can tell him a story. That's what you do for me when I don't feel good. It always makes me feel better."

The sweet offer nearly brought tears to Brianna's eyes, and she did her best to hold them back. Having Ruthie see her cry would only raise more questions.

"I think he just needs some quiet time."

"Oh." Ruthie thought about it. "Quiet time is good. Except when I've done something bad and you say that I need to have time-out. It's quiet time, but it's not good." The memory made her mouth turn down, but it didn't stay that way for long. "I'm glad Gideon isn't in trouble."

Brianna waded through that explanation of good quiet times and bad ones. It made her smile, which she sorely needed.

Was there a way she could make Gideon smile? It would take more than one of Ruthie's explanations, though. His spirit had taken a huge blow with Nate's death.

How much time did he need before he was ready to accept her sympathy? Should she go to him, insist that he talk about it? Or did she respect the closed door between them?

In the end, she knew she needed to let him come to her in his own time. When he was ready to talk, she'd be there.

But she couldn't forget the bleakness in his eyes or the pain in his voice when he'd told her about Nate.

When it was time for Ruthie to go down for a nap, she gave an exhausted sigh and then did what she always did when everything seemed stacked against her.

She got to her knees. And prayed.

Gideon did his best to keep his grief inside, but it leaked through despite his efforts. The tears he refused to shed were born of pain and loss and helplessness.

Exhaustion had piled onto the grief until he could barely put two words together. He knew Brianna would listen, wanted to listen, wanted to help, but how did he explain the loss?

Nate was his brother in every way that counted. They'd gone through BUD/S together and kept each other from ringing the bell that said "I quit" when the freezing water, lack of sleep and grueling runs with 90-pound packs grew too much.

They'd kept each other going through the last week of training when ninety percent of the class dropped out, unable to run and swim ten miles a day with less than five hours sleep for the entire week.

They were among the ten percent who finished, recognizing that it wasn't physical stature or conditioning that distinguished those who made it from those who didn't. It was the ability to see something larger than yourself and then be willing to work toward achieving it. They'd endured the physical, mental and emotional challenges and understood the mission of the SEALs: to accomplish the op and to take care of each other.

Not only had he and Nate trained together, but they'd also fought together, and saved each other's lives on more than one occasion. There was no grandstanding in the SEALs, no lone-wolf heroics. The mission depended upon teamwork.

Once you'd shared being prisoners of war, enduring the worst that one man could inflict upon another, there was little that you didn't know about your brother. When things had gotten too bad, he and Nate had cried together and then eventually had escaped together. No SEAL left a buddy behind.

Losing him was like losing a limb, something so integral to his being that he wondered if he could ever function again.

Head bowed in grief, he remained sitting for long minutes. When he got to his feet, it was with steely resolve. He'd find who had killed his friend. Find them and make them pay. Now that he'd put some distance between himself and the killing, Gideon had time to think and the obvious question had surfaced: *What had happened?*

A killer hadn't just come across Nate and him. Either Nate had been followed, or he, Gideon, had. He was betting on it being Nate. Gideon had checked and double-checked for tails, taking SDRs the entire way.

Not for the first time, he accepted that someone in the marshals was a traitor.

The knowledge chilled him. It chilled him right down to the bone.

He found Brianna checking her and Ruthie's duffel bags.

"We've got some decisions to make," he said.

"About leaving here?"

He nodded. "I don't know that we've been compromised, but I don't know that we haven't been."

It was a poor way to describe their circumstances, but it was all that he had.

"We're safe here. For now," she said. "I can't see pulling out of here when we don't know where the next threat's coming from."

She was right.

Her calm assessment was exactly why he'd sought her out.

"Thanks. Anyone ever tell you that you could have had a career in the diplomatic corps?"

"No." She gave an emphatic shake of her head. "If it's anything like making nice with the higher-ups who came to give their suggestions to the marshals, count me out."

That raised a grin from him. "Same here."

The minute of banter felt good. He'd needed that. With her innate kindness, Brianna had sensed that and had given him a slice of humanity.

Her sensitivity was only one of the things he admired about her. It reminded him that her beauty went far beyond the surface and reached deep down inside.

Only one day had passed since they'd reached the cabin. In some ways, it seemed like far more. In others, it seemed that only a few hours had passed. He was ever mindful of the danger they faced from further attacks.

The blizzard was a nasty one, all teeth and claws of wind and snow and cold, but he couldn't trust it alone to protect them. He had precious cargo to safeguard.

NINE

Ruthie bounded in just then. "Mommy, can we make snow angels?"

Brianna looked to Gideon. "Can we?" She understood the threat they were under, but, at the same time, wanted a small pocket of fun for Ruthie. And, she admitted, for herself.

He glanced out the window. "For a little while. Before the wind picks up any more."

The three of them didn't last ten minutes making snow angels before the wind and cold drove them back inside, but it was enough to satisfy Ruthie. Brianna smiled at the picture she made: red-cheeked, with ice crystals clinging to her lashes.

She shielded her eyes from the ever-falling snow, thinking that the snow angels looked like a family. Father, mother, child. It felt like they were in their own little snow globe where no one could hurt them.

The fanciful notion caused her to smile. The

smile quickly died, though, as she realized it wasn't true. Jameson had proven how easily he could reach them.

Inside the cabin, Brianna ushered her daughter to the bathroom. "It's a warm bath and dry clothes for you."

"Wasn't this the funnest time ever?" Ruthie asked.

With snow down the neck of her parka and hands numb with cold, Brianna did her best to agree.

Teeth chattering, Ruthie turned to Gideon. "I like making s-snow angels. Don't you, Gideon?"

"There's no one I'd rather make snow angels with than you," he said and lifted her into his arms to swing around.

"You're a good sport," Brianna whispered after he'd put Ruthie down and she'd scampered off to the bedroom. "Thank you." She knew he hadn't wanted them outside the cabin, but he'd taken them out to appease Ruthie, all the while keeping watch over them. Warmth flooded through her at the patience and tenderness he showed to her daughter. And for the briefest of moments, she pictured herself, Gideon and Ruthie as a family.

Ruthlessly, she banished the image. It had no place in her life, but she couldn't deny the pang in her heart as she accepted that truth.

Twenty minutes later, freshly showered under

water as hot as she could stand and dressed in flannel-lined jeans, an Under Armour long-sleeved T-shirt and a heavy sweater, she felt almost human again. Ruthie was already in fleecy pajamas.

They found Gideon in the kitchen.

"Is that what I think it is?" Brianna asked, sniffing appreciatively.

He threw a teasing look her way. "What do you think it is?"

"It smells like hot chocolate. With cinnamon. Just the way I like it."

"Got it in one."

"Does it have little marshmallows?" Ruthie asked.

He looked affronted. "Of course. You can't have hot chocolate without little marshmallows."

A few minutes later, the three of them sipped the hot drink.

Ruthie smacked her lips. "Can I have seconds?"

In answer, Gideon refilled her mug.

"Thank you," Brianna said. "For everything." Did he know that she was thanking him for more than hot chocolate?

The blizzard was a fierce one. Wind whipped branches against the windows, the thud of wood smacking glass reverberating throughout the house. Gideon wasn't concerned about supplies or heat. The cabin was stocked with a good supply of food and plenty of propane and firewood.

They wouldn't starve or freeze to death. No, that wasn't the danger. The danger lay in those who were seeking them. He knew the men searching for Brianna and her daughter wouldn't be put off forever by a blizzard, no matter how bad.

Men like that only hunkered down and forced their way through any obstacles. In that way, they were much like SEALs and other special operators. However, those in the spec-ops community worked to bring about justice and, where they could, peace. It wasn't that they were perfect— far from it—but they saw their job as a mission to help those who couldn't help themselves.

Gideon had no illusions about himself. He was quick-tempered and inclined to dole out his own brand of justice upon occasion, but his training had tempered those tendencies and had made him a better man and a better operator for it.

And though the isolation was a blessing at the moment, if a threat appeared, he and Brianna were on their own.

Snow blanketed the ground and coated the trees, but now it had turned to sleet, the ice pellets tapping against the cabin. Other than that, there was nothing but a groaning silence.

He checked the doors and windows—again—then stirred the dying embers in the fireplace to life. Brianna was curled up on the sofa in front of the fire. He pictured the two of them nestled on the sofa, Ruthie and Miso snuggled in with them.

He shook his head to clear it of the image, but it persisted. There was too much history between them for that particular picture to become a reality.

Brianna looked up, a tiny frown between her eyebrows. "Couldn't sleep?"

"Too much on my mind," he said. "What are you doing up at this hour?"

"Same." Her smile invited him to join her.

He sat next to her. Close enough to smell the scent of her hair, but not too close. He longed to reach out and take her hand in his. Instead, he let his own rest on the cushion next to hers.

He caught her looking at the two hands, almost touching, but not quite.

"When this is over," he said, "what will you and Ruthie do?"

"Go back to Silverton. Pick up our lives." Her smile slipped a bit. "If we can. What about you?"

"Go back to work at—" He paused. A movement from outside reflected in the window caught his attention. He pushed her to the floor. "There's someone out there."

"In this weather?"

He didn't bother answering. "Stay low and get to Ruthie. This can't be good." The figure had disappeared, but Gideon knew he hadn't imagined it.

Someone was watching.

Brianna knew that Gideon wanted to take the fight to whoever was out there because he didn't want them anywhere near her or Ruthie. While she appreciated that, she doubted that the intruder had come alone. There were probably two or more of them.

She didn't want to leave Gideon to deal with Jameson's men on his own, but she didn't have a choice. She had to see to Ruthie. Her safety came first. Always.

But maybe there was something she could do to help.

"I'll take care of us. It's you I'm worried about," she said. "If someone came for us in this weather, he's not going to go down easy." Either the assailants were foolhardy in the extreme or had total confidence in their ability to take out her and Gideon.

"I'll be all right. Keep your weapon close. Just in case."

"Just in case." She understood what he meant. *Just in case someone got past him.* And if they did, it meant Gideon had been killed. Her voice trembled, but her chin remained firm. "Stay safe."

"Always."

She watched as he slipped into the night, and her heart clutched. She refused to waste a moment worrying. She had things to do. Things like protecting her daughter.

She hurried to the bedroom, where Ruthie sat up in her bed, rubbing her eyes sleepily. "Mommy? Is something wrong?"

"A bad man has found us. Are your things ready to go?"

Ruthie nodded. "In my backpack."

When Brianna checked the backpack, her fingers encountered an unfamiliar object. A nearly invisible disc was attached to the bottom of the pack. It felt like plastic, but closer inspection showed it to be some kind of filament, so thin that when she pulled it off, it nearly slipped through her fingers.

So this was how they were being tracked. When the men tried to abduct Ruthie a number of days ago—had it only been days?—one of them must have slipped this onto her backpack. It would have taken only a second to do so. If only she'd discovered it sooner.

Her daughter's face scrunched into a frown. "Do we have to leave?"

"I'm afraid so."

"I like it here." The frown deepened. "Miso likes it, too."

"So do I." Brianna spared a moment to hold her daughter close. A too-wise expression filled Ruthie's eyes. "Do I have to get in the bathtub again?"

Brianna nodded. She wouldn't lie to her daughter. "The bad men are outside right now. If they get in the house, I want you to be safe."

Ruthie looked doubtful. Brianna couldn't blame her, but the tub was the best place to be if bullets started flying.

"I'll be back," she promised.

"Mommy?"

"Yes?"

"Be safe. Keep Miso safe, too."

"I will."

Brianna settled Miso on top of a blanket in the corner of the bedroom and headed to the kitchen, where she set a pot of water to boil. She hadn't filled the pot all the way full; she wanted it light enough that she could fling the contents at an intruder if need be. After she slipped a kitchen knife into her boot, she moved the block of knives into a lower cabinet.

Preparedness on all fronts.

Her Walther at the back of her waistband, she prepared to face the enemy.

Bundled in a Patagonia jacket, Gideon made his way to the barn. He ran various options through his mind, trying to think what he would do if he was intent on killing everyone inside the cabin. Without knowing whom he was facing, he could only speculate.

Much of it depended upon how many men were out here. Was there only one, or a team of two or four? Or even more?

The intruder could stage a frontal attack, blast through the front door with an explosive. That would have the element of surprise, but there were risks associated with it.

No, if he was staging the op, he'd find another way in. The side door, or a window in an unoccupied room. The weather would play a big part in any plans. The assassin would have to have a place to hole up in the cold. No one could survive for long in this weather without shelter.

If someone had been spying on them, it was likely he'd taken shelter in the barn in between spells of surveillance.

It was then he saw it tucked in a copse of trees at the side of the cabin—a burly 4x4 with huge tires that could navigate any kind of terrain and weather. No wonder the assailants had been able to make it here.

Gideon looked for tracks and, within a few minutes, found them. He'd been right. Snowshoe tracks led to and away from the barn. As far as he could tell, the most recent tracks went back to the barn.

It could be a trick. An experienced assassin would know how to lay down a false trail.

Gideon tried to walk in the tracks, but with the snow nearly waist deep, that was impossible. He slipped to the side with every other step, leaving an unmistakable set of different tracks.

With as much stealth as possible, he opened the barn door, grateful it didn't squeak, then inched along the wall. The darkness was so absolute that he couldn't make out anything and called upon his memory to navigate the blackness. Over there, to the right, was the tractor he'd bought and rarely used, and to the left—

A muted footfall alerted him to movement. He'd been right. The intruder had holed up in the barn.

The darkness now his friend, he moved toward the sound. He turned his breathing shallow, the sound barely a whisper in his ear. He relied upon the instincts honed by dozens of special-ops assignments to identify the man's location.

A foreign smell, one that didn't belong in a barn, reached him. That told him one of two things. Either the assassin wasn't as experienced as he thought—a well-trained soldier knew to obliterate any scent while tracking a prey, including soap—or the man had been pressed into duty quickly and hadn't had time to fully prepare.

He remained perfectly still, then spun and

kicked his leg in a wide arc. When it landed against an unyielding object, he knew he'd scored a hit.

An *ooomph* of pain confirmed it, but his opponent wasn't down. A fist shot out, catching Gideon on the jaw.

Okay.

Player identified. Now came the real match.

The men sparred in the darkness. His foe was well-trained, used his hands and feet like he'd been in the military.

The two men grappled with each other, grunting and huffing in the frigid air. When Gideon got hold of the man's jacket, he noticed that it wasn't wet. It was cold, but not wet, as though he'd recently been outside. He wasn't the man Gideon had seen in the window.

It was then that he realized he'd miscalculated. Badly.

The man hadn't come alone. He had a partner, one who was even now probably sneaking up on the house or perhaps was already inside.

The shock of it caused him to lose a beat, giving his enemy the opportunity to grab a weapon and get off a shot. The noise reverberated through the otherwise silent barn, though it wasn't as loud as might be expected.

This was no ordinary weapon.

Pain burned from his upper arm down to his

fingers. Gideon grunted and pressed his hand to the wound. Though he couldn't see it, he knew that his gloved hand came away bloody. The wound wouldn't kill him, but it would slow his reaction time, maybe by only a few seconds, but that could be the difference between surviving and dying.

With his good arm, Gideon put all his power into a jab aimed at his enemy's jaw. It connected and dropped him cold. After sparing a few seconds to undo the man's belt and hogtie his hands and feet, he grabbed the gun.

Brianna. Ruthie.

He had to get to them.

He half ran, half dragged himself through the deep snow. It didn't matter that he was bleeding. It didn't matter that he was growing numb from the cold. Nothing mattered but getting to the mother and daughter entrusted to his care.

Nothing.

TEN

The sound of breaking glass alerted Brianna that a tango, military slang for the enemy, had found his way inside. He wasn't trying to disguise the noise, no doubt confident in his ability to take out her and Gideon.

His arrogance was going to cost him.

She wanted to sneak up behind him. She couldn't let him get anywhere near Ruthie. Weapon in hand, she approached with all the stealth she could bring to bear, but something must have given her away.

He spun and kicked the Walther from her hand, the force of the motion nearly knocking her over. She flung out her arms to keep her balance.

Okay.

She could handle this. She crouched, presenting a smaller target for the flying hands and feet he sent her way. When she saw her opening, she seized it. She came in low and caught him with a sharp one-two punch to the gut.

The surprise on his face would have been comical if it hadn't been immediately replaced with rage, making her think he was one of those men who didn't like having a woman show him up. Well, she'd dealt with that type before.

She'd do it again.

"You're going to hurt before this is over," he said, his bushy eyebrows crashing together. "You're going to hurt real bad."

"I won't be the only one," she retorted. She sliced a leg through the air to connect with his kneecap, then followed up with a blow to the bridge of his nose. Her fist came away aching from the impact, but she wasn't the only one in pain. Blood spurted from his nose, and he had to pause to wipe it away.

Murder in his eyes, he started toward her but was stopped by an unexpected ally.

Miso climbed up his leg, sharp little claws digging into fabric and perhaps even flesh. She hissed, baring her teeth. With an angry mutter, he shook off the cat, but the attack had slowed him down for half a minute.

Brianna took advantage of that and delivered a roundhouse kick to his chest. It did its job and sent him sprawling to the floor, but he jumped up immediately. Leading him to the surprise she had waiting, she dashed into the kitchen.

When she judged the distance right, she hurled the pot of boiling water at him.

Face scalded, he let out an ear-shattering screech, burst through the glass door and threw himself into the snow, shouting invectives at her the entire time.

Before she could get to him, he pushed himself up and started running. She started to chase after him when she saw Gideon, clutching his arm, staggering toward her. She ran to help him into the house, then hurried to check on Ruthie before returning to see to his wounds.

As gently as possible, she helped him to a kitchen chair and removed his jacket and flannel shirt. She snipped through his T-shirt, exposing the wound. Seeing that it continued to bleed freely, she cleaned it, then pressed a cloth over it.

"You need to go to a hospital."

"We're not going anywhere tonight," he said. "Besides, it's just a graze." But the pain-filled lines radiating from the corners of his eyes told her that it was more than a slight graze. From the look of it, the bullet had dug a piece of flesh from his arm.

"There's something else we need to do." He led the way to the barn where he pointed to a man lying on his side, trussed up, hands and feet bound together. "I want answers from him."

She hunkered down at the man's side, ready

to question him, when Gideon groaned, causing her to turn and look up at him.

She wanted to interrogate their prisoner now, but Gideon was pale and breathing hard. She had to get him back to the cabin before he couldn't walk on his own. On impulse, she searched the man and found a set of keys. Thinking they might come in handy, she pocketed them.

Back inside the cabin, she gently pushed him to a chair, grabbed a throw from the back of the sofa, and put it over him.

He closed his eyes.

She took the opportunity to check on Ruthie. Bless her, the little girl had slept through everything.

Brianna said a silent prayer of gratitude, thanking the Lord for bringing them through this. She knew they would have to leave here soon, but she hoped they had a few hours. Gideon desperately needed the rest, and, truth be told, so did she, but she couldn't afford to let down her guard. She found a piece of particleboard to cover the shattered glass door and nailed it in place. The process exhausted her all over again, but it had to be done. However much longer they stayed here, she couldn't leave the huge hole as it was.

In between that and checking on Gideon, there wasn't much opportunity for her to rest. Gideon's color was better, as was his breathing. She checked the doors and windows again, then went to her and Ruthie's room. After lifting Ruthie from the tub, she placed her in bed and took a chair across from it, her weapon in her lap.

Gideon awoke to pain.

He registered it, then compartmentalized it, as he'd learned. Pain was only one factor in a myriad of others and couldn't be allowed to dominate his thoughts. Not now. Not when he and Brianna and Ruthie had to get out of here.

He knew that when Jameson didn't hear back from his men in a reasonable amount of time, he'd send others. And others after that.

With some difficulty, Gideon got to his feet, steadied himself. Okay, he wasn't back to full speed yet, but he could function.

It was then he smelled the smoke coming from the far side of the front room, its acrid smell burning his nose.

He hurried to Brianna and Ruthie's room and woke Brianna. "Fire. We have to get out of here. Now," he said. "Get Ruthie and Miso. Forget the bags."

Gideon wrapped Ruthie in a blanket. By now, the flames had engulfed most of the front room There was no way to get on the other side of the flames but to fight their way through them.

"Go," he ordered Brianna. "I'll be right behind you."

She cradled Miso to her and ran through the flames.

Gideon hunched over Ruthie, doing his best to protect her from the worst of the heat.

Within seconds, though it seemed far longer, they were through. The cabin went up quickly, the flames eating away through the cedar siding with hungry bites of fire and fury.

His arms burned under the strain of carrying Ruthie, but he didn't slow down. Would his truck make it through the blizzard? Then he recalled the assailants' vehicle.

He pointed to the 4x4 and shouted over the wind. "It's our best bet of making it out of the valley, but we need the keys."

To his amazement, Brianna pulled a set of keys from her pocket. How had she managed that?

"But we need Ruthie's car seat," she shouted back.

He was tempted to shout over the sounds of the fire and blizzard that there was someone on the property, trying to burn them out or shoot them. Or both. Did it really matter if Ruthie was in her car seat?

One look at the resolution in Brianna's face told him yes, it mattered.

Fortunately the snow and cold kept the fire

from reaching the barn. With Ruthie over his good shoulder, he unlatched the doors.

Brianna got the car seat, and they then fought their way through the wind and snow to the 4x4, where she strapped the car seat into the back seat and settled Ruthie in it, Miso beside her.

"What about the man tied up in the barn?" she asked.

"He's safe enough for now. I'll send someone back for him."

After buckling their safety belts around themselves, they took off with Brianna behind the wheel.

The narrow mountain road was treacherously slick, ice coating the surface. When they reached the highway, she upped the speed and took off down the mostly abandoned road. When they encountered a patch of ice, she wrestled with the steering wheel, struggling to right the car's direction. Just as it appeared they were going to go off the road, she brought it back around.

"Thank You, God."

Brianna's nearly silent words reached him.

"You still believe."

"Always. I have to."

"Even after all you've been through?" He made a question out of the words.

"Especially after all I've been through. Without the Lord, I would have given up long ago.

When I was growing up, my parents were missionaries. We moved frequently and sometimes had to leave a lot our belongings behind, but one thing that always came with us was a wall hanging my mother had embroidered that read, 'Oh Lord of infinite patience, here I am again.'"

"I envy your belief."

"It can be yours. All you have to do is take that first step and acknowledge that the Lord is there and that He loves you."

"I want to," he said honestly.

"Start there."

He didn't answer. He didn't know if he could take that step. "You make it sound easy."

"It is. But it takes courage." She gave him a long look. "I never thought you were afraid of anything."

He hadn't thought so, either. It turned out that he was wrong.

After six hours on the road, Brianna slid Gideon a sidelong glance, reading the worry in his eyes. They hadn't encountered any tangos since fleeing the cabin, so she didn't think it was that that caused his anxiety.

Thinking she could relieve at least one of the worries he carried, she told him about the filament she'd found on Ruthie's backpack.

"So that's how they did it," he said. Weariness filled his voice.

"I'm afraid so."

"What did you do with it?"

"Left it there."

"I wondered how Jameson's people kept finding us, especially after I turned the minivan inside out when we were at the gas station."

"Ruthie had her backpack with her when we went to the restroom." If only they'd known. "No sense crying over what can't be helped."

To her surprise, Gideon smiled. "I've missed that about you."

"What?"

"Your practicality."

"I've had to be practical."

His smile died as abruptly as it had appeared. "We can't keep Ruthie with us any longer." His voice was quiet, but the words reverberated through her with heart-shattering intensity.

Brianna had been waiting for this, and even though she'd thought the same thing, she wanted to rail against it. "But where can I take her? It's not like I can just call up a friend to take care of her." She winced at her bitter tone. "We don't have any friends, especially ones who are willing to take in a child who could be a target."

"I know some people. The Zunigas. Friends at

S and J. They'll take care of her and guard her with their lives if it became necessary."

"Why? Why would they do that for someone they don't even know?"

"That's the kind of people they are."

Preparing Ruthie to leave was the hardest thing Brianna had ever done. They'd never been separated. Never. Not even overnight, though Ruthie had once begged to have a sleepover at her friend Lily's.

"I don't want to do this," Brianna said. "I don't want to leave you. But I need to keep you safe." Did her daughter know that it was tearing the heart from her?

"From the bad men?" Ruthie asked.

"From the bad men."

Her daughter understood more than she should. Too much more. What five-year-old should know that she and her mother were on the run from killers?

Brianna searched for something more to say, something reassuring, something profound. But the only words she could find were "I love you."

"I love you back."

The drive to the Zunigas' ranch on the outskirts of the town of Shadow Point was quiet. So very quiet. Without having to employ multiple SDRs and being chased by Jameson's goons, it was a much shorter drive than that to the cabin.

Brianna wanted to fill it with chatter, but she couldn't find any words that didn't sound clichéd or foolishly cheerful. Ruthie sat in her car seat, her expression solemn. Each time Brianna turned to look at her daughter, her heart hiccupped in her chest, a tiny little blip that sounded as mournful as she felt.

Shannon and Rafe Zuniga may have been the most beautiful couple Brianna had ever seen. Shannon was slender, delicate, but with a tensile strength that said that though she might bend, she would never break. And Rafe was dark-haired and dark-eyed, and towered above her. The love that passed between them spoke of an unshakeable bond, one forged by commitment and faith.

A moment of envy raised its head as Brianna acknowledged that that was what she'd lacked with Jack.

Gideon grasped Rafe's hand, gave Shannon a brotherly hug and then made the introductions, including Miso.

"Miso. What a fine name for a cat," Shannon said. "It suits her."

"Miso is my best friend," Ruthie said. "Well, after Mommy."

Rafe hunkered down to peer at Miso through her carrier before settling a large hand on Ruthie's shoulder. "I hope you'll let Shannon and me be your friends, too."

Ruthie's face took on what Brianna privately called her "considering" pose. "I'll think about it."

The four adults did their best to stifle their laughter.

When it came time to say goodbye, Brianna nearly broke down, but she kept her voice light, her smile in place. "I'll be back as soon as I can."

Ruthie clung to her. "I don't want you to leave, Mommy."

Brianna looked up at Gideon, praying for an alternative to hunting down killers while still keeping Ruthie safe. The gravity in his gaze told her there was no other way.

"I have to leave you," she said, leaning down to be on Ruthie's level and drawing her close. The flutter of her daughter's eyelashes against her cheek nearly did her in. "But only for a short time. Then I'll be back and give you so many hugs that you won't be able to count them."

Ruthie pulled back and gave Brianna a searching look. "Will it help you and Gideon catch the bad men if you leave me?"

"Yes," Brianna said honestly. "It will."

"Then it's all right. If you catch them, then they can't hurt anyone else."

"That's right." Brianna looked at her daughter, who was wise beyond her years. "I love you. I'll always love you."

Ruthie fixed her attention on Gideon. "Do you promise to keep Mommy safe?"

He kneeled so that he was at eye level with her. "I promise."

"Shake on it," she said and stuck out a tiny hand.

He took her hand in his, his deeply tanned fingers wrapping around hers. He pulled something from his pocket and pressed it in her hand. "This is my SEAL unit's coin. It's given when a soldier has shown exceptional bravery. Like you have. You never once complained when the bad men were chasing us."

Ruthie held out the coin for Brianna to see. "Look, Mommy. Isn't it beautiful?"

"Beautiful," she agreed, her gaze finding Gideon's. *Thank you*, she mouthed over her daughter's head.

"I'm not worried anymore, Mommy," Ruthie said. "Gideon promised to keep you safe, and he wouldn't go back on a promise."

He stood and swept Ruthie up in his arms. She wrapped her arms around his neck.

Brianna held back the tears stinging her eyes at the picture the big man and small girl made.

When he set her down, Shannon held out a hand. "Ruthie, we have llamas on our property. Would you like to pet one? They're usually friendly." She made a face. "Except when they spit. Then you'd better watch out."

Ruthie's eyes grew wide. "I never petted a llama." With one last hug for Brianna, she took Shannon's outstretched hand.

Brianna watched as Ruthie and Shannon headed toward a barn. She lifted her gaze to Rafe. "I can't thank you enough for doing this. Not everyone would take in a child they don't know."

Rafe, whom Gideon had said had a heart as big as he was, gazed at her in compassion. "We'll keep her safe," he promised, his dark eyes filled with understanding. "Gideon's a friend, so that makes you a friend, too. Friends help each other out."

Tears stung her eyes. Friends had been in short supply in her life during the last six years. Shannon and Rafe had just met her, but they'd accepted her and Ruthie without question.

"Thank you."

Shannon rejoined them then. "Ruthie's with Hannah, one of our ranch hands," she said, obviously reading the concern in Brianna's eyes. "Hey, tears are only allowed if they're happy ones, and we're happy to have Ruthie here. She's welcome to stay as long as you need."

"She likes a night-light on when she goes to bed. Miso usually sleeps in the bed with her, but if that's a problem—"

"We live on a ranch with three dogs, six llamas and four goats who will eat your shoelaces and everything else," Shannon said. "I think we can handle one little cat."

"Miso can have an attitude when she wants to."

"That's fine. There's nothing I like better than a cat with cat-itude."

And with that, Brianna knew Ruthie and Miso were going to be just fine. Still, leaving her daughter was one of the hardest things she had ever had to do. Scratch that. Make it *the* hardest thing she'd ever had to do.

Even knowing it was for Ruthie's protection, leaving her daughter clawed at her heart. As they got farther and farther away from the ranch, she longed to tell Gideon to turn back, to take Ruthie with them, and run until no one could find them.

ELEVEN

Gideon didn't try to talk Brianna out of her feelings. What must it feel like to leave her child behind, even when it was to protect her? He didn't try to pretend he understood. When she wanted to talk, he'd be there. In the meantime, he'd give her the time and space she needed.

She held herself stiffly, as though afraid if she relaxed even a fraction, her feelings would spill over. He understood her enough to know that she wasn't one to give way to her emotions. Not if she could help it.

"The Zunigas seem like a great couple," she said at last.

"They are. They didn't have an easy time of it at first, but they've made a good life for themselves."

"Does Rafe work with you?"

Gideon nodded. "We're fortunate to have him. He's a first-class operative."

"And Shannon?"

"She's a DDA in the Shadow Point DA's office. They met when she was receiving threats and he was assigned to protect her."

He knew Brianna needed to be reassured that Rafe and Shannon would keep Ruthie safe, so he recounted Rafe's prowess with every conceivable weapon and Shannon's skill in hand-to-hand combat. They were supremely qualified to protect the little girl.

"It'll never come to that, though," Gideon said. "No one will know where Ruthie is. She's safe. Shannon and Rafe won't let anything happen to her."

"I know. But…"

"I get it. She's your daughter."

"She's my *everything*. And I'll worry about her no matter where she is or who she's with. It goes with the territory."

"You made the right decision," Gideon said. "She wasn't safe when she was with us."

"I know. If something happened to her, I don't know what I'd do." Her voice cracked on the last word.

"It won't. We're going to get Jameson and the rest of his crew and put them away where they'll never hurt anyone again."

What few words they exchanged after that were stilted, and he realized how much Ruthie had eased the tension between them with her constant questions and on-the-spot insights. Awkward silence, made even more so by the attraction he'd always felt toward Brianna, now filled the air.

Did she feel it, too? Or was it all on his side? He couldn't very well ask her.

Another realization hit him. He missed Ruthie. She had found her way into his heart. How could she not? She was bright, curious and funny. If he had a daughter, he'd want her to be like Ruthie.

Startled at the thought, he exhaled a long breath. Where had that come from?

He'd never thought of having a family of his own. His home life had been a dark place; he never wanted to inflict such pain on an innocent child.

The only light had been his time at school, where he'd devoured books and every bit of learning he could digest.

No, he didn't have it in him to be the kind of father a sensitive child like Ruthie needed. She and Brianna needed stability and the kind of love that lasted a lifetime. Whatever he felt for mother and daughter had to remain unspoken. Brianna didn't need the stress of dealing with his feelings for her.

He threw a glance her way, noted the shadows beneath her eyes, so dark that they looked like bruises on her fair skin. "Why don't you rest for a little while? We've got a ways to go."

When she didn't ask where they were going, he realized how much saying goodbye to Ruthie had taken out of her. His heart twisted at the anguish he read on her face.

She followed his advice and closed her eyes.

When her breathing leveled out and her chest rose and fell evenly, he thought of his promise to Ruthie to keep her mother safe. Never had a promise meant more to him.

The motel appeared worse for wear—tiny rooms strung together like paste gems on a tawdry necklace. Like many lodgings that speckled the roads leading to and from the mountains, it had only the most basic of amenities.

Brianna didn't mind the modest accommodations. They were clean, quiet and, best of all, no one had followed them. Unlike the cabin, it wasn't far from town and would make a convenient home base.

After discovering the tracker attached to Ruthie's backpack, she had felt relatively confident in not being followed, but that didn't mean they didn't take precautions. Only a fool was careless. They still looked over their shoulders with every move.

One of the adjoining rooms boasted a kitchenette, which meant they didn't have to go out for meals.

When Gideon's phone chirped, she nearly jumped. He'd told her that only Nate had the number, so who was calling him now?

Her startled gaze met Gideon's. He put it on speaker mode, and Brianna listened carefully. "Yes?"

"Toria Callahan." The low voice had a no-nonsense quality to it.

"How did you get this number?"

"We recovered Nate Saxton's phone. This number was in it. Am I speaking to Gideon Stratham?"

Gideon's gaze met Brianna's. She nodded. "Yes."

"We need to meet."

"Why?"

"So we can exchange information."

"Why can't we do it over the phone?" he asked.

"I don't share intel over the phone. Not with my people. Not with anyone."

Another nod. "Okay. But I pick the time and place."

"Fair enough."

They settled upon a time, and Gideon told her he'd text her the location later.

"Do you think we can trust her?" Brianna asked once he'd hung up.

"I think we don't have a choice. We need information. Without Nate, we're operating blind."

The meeting time was in two hours. Gideon and Brianna arrived at the designated spot early. He didn't text Callahan the location of the meeting place until the last minute, a tactic of which Brianna approved. Both Gideon and Brianna were carrying, their weapons tucked at the back of their waists for easy access, and though he'd liked to have had the rifle he took off the gunman in the barn at his cabin, he couldn't very well carry it into the diner. He'd left it locked in their vehicle.

The hole-in-the-wall diner was off the beaten track, which was precisely why he'd chosen it. The place was shabby, but the red vinyl booths promised comfort, and the smells coming from the kitchen were enticing. Her stomach rumbled at the thought of food, reminding her that they hadn't had anything to eat since before they'd left Ruthie with the Zunigas.

Brianna couldn't help but smile as Gideon attracted the attention of every female diner. In his Filson vest to ward off the cold, flannel shirt and Levi's, he was dressed like many other men in the state, except for the boots. Rather than the ubiquitous cowboy boots, he wore Oakley combat boots. The boots were scarred and weathered, the rough wear speaking of a man who lived hard and worked hard.

But it wasn't just his good looks that had

women giving him a once-over. It was the air of confidence that he exuded, made all the more appealing because he didn't trade on it. To the uninitiated, he looked like any man gifted with self-assurance. However, those with a trained eye noticed how he was hyperaware of everything and everyone about him.

That situational awareness was part of what had made him so good at his job with the marshals. He saw everything without appearing to pay particular notice to anything. Picking up on the smallest detail could mean the difference between life and death.

Satisfied that no tangos were in the vicinity, they settled in a booth, both with their backs to the wall. She took the opportunity to study the man who had risked his life time and time again for her and Ruthie.

She knew he was running hot right now, meaning that every one of his senses was switched on. She doubted a fly could land on the waiter's shoulder without him being aware of it.

"You can relax," she said. "I've checked it out." Without calling attention to it, she'd done a visual grid search of the diner. Only two other customers were present—two seventyish men who looked like they'd already spent a few hours there and weren't planning on leaving anytime soon.

"Who says I'm not relaxed?"

"I do." She began ticking off her points on her fingers. "You're sitting with your back to the wall. You removed your weapon from the back of your waist, and your right hand is clutching it under the table while your left hand is drumming a beat on the table."

"First, I always sit with my back to the wall, just like you. That's just good sense."

She acknowledged that with a dip of her head.

"Second, you don't know that my right hand is clutching my piece under the table."

"Is it?" she challenged.

"That's not the point. Third," he continued without missing a step, "if I'm tapping on the table, it's because I'm waiting for our meet to arrive."

"It's all right," she said.

"Thanks." His dry tone let her know that he wasn't really annoyed. But he was worried. She saw it in the lines that bracketed his mouth. "We should never have agreed to this. At the very least, I should have left you behind. You're a target."

"You're a target, too, if you remember," she pointed out. "Jameson wants both of us dead after he gets what he wants."

"But I'm the one who's supposed to be watching over you. Not the other way around."

"Does it really make a difference who's supposed to be watching who?" She frowned. "Whom."

The tiny smile in his eyes lightened the worry

in her heart by a fraction. "You choose now to worry about grammar?"

"What can I say?" She lifted a shoulder. "I'm a grammar nerd."

"Thanks."

"For what?"

"For trying to take my mind off what's going on."

"Did it work?"

"A little. Enough for me to realize I can't solve this all by myself."

She reached for his hand.

He gave her fingers a gentle squeeze. The smile flickered out. "I don't like waiting. We're too exposed here. The danger could come from anyplace, anyone."

She watched as, always vigilant, he shifted his gaze from one side of the diner to the other and back again before zeroing in on a young waiter who looked like he had yet to shave.

"We'll have to keep an eye on him," she said with a straight face. "He looks like a serious bad guy."

"Okay, so maybe I'm a bit paranoid."

"Just a bit. You said yourself that we needed more info. That means we have to talk with people."

He nodded without taking his attention away from the movement in the diner.

When Toria Callahan showed up with another marshal accompanying her, Brianna kept her surprise to herself. There'd been no mention of bringing anyone with her. Berrot Newhouse, a marshal whom she'd known back in the day, smiled briefly.

"Berrot," she said.

He acknowledged the greeting with a half-smile.

Before she and Jack had started dating, she and Newhouse had gone out together briefly. There'd been no spark, at least on her part, and she'd been relieved to end what had been a very short relationship. They'd never worked together, but he'd had a good rep in the US Marshals Service.

"Toria Callahan," the woman said and stuck out a hand.

Brianna took it and approved of the firm grip. She had never had any direct dealings with Callahan, but had heard good things about her. She made a note of the woman's Cucinelli cashmere coat. Its price alone would put Ruthie through a year of college. Maybe two.

The woman turned to Gideon. "You know Newhouse." The two men shook hands. "We have a leak," she said after she and Newhouse sat opposite them. "Nate must have told you. I need to know what else he told you before he died. It's critical."

The woman didn't waste time with pleasantries. Brianna approved of that, too.

Gideon didn't answer right away. When he did speak, his words were measured. "He'd told me earlier that he suspected a leak in the marshals. He didn't have time to say anything more the night he was killed."

"You're certain?" Urgency underscored Callahan's words. "Nothing at all?"

"That's right."

"I can't stress how important this is."

"I know just how important it is," Gideon said in an even tone. "Nate gave his life to the marshals and for what he believed."

Callahan spent a few moments sizing him up.

"If Stratham says he doesn't have anything, then he doesn't have anything," Newhouse said to break the silence. "He's a straight arrow."

"Thanks, man."

Brianna watched the exchange between the two men. If Gideon thought Newhouse was okay, then she'd accept that. Just because she hadn't clicked with him didn't mean that he wasn't a good marshal.

She sat back, content to watch the exchange between the two marshals and Gideon.

Gideon leaned in. "What can *you* tell *me*?" he asked, his gaze encompassing both Callahan and Newhouse.

Callahan folded her arms across her chest. "I came here to get information, not to give it to a civilian."

"I wasn't always a civilian," he pointed out.

"No, but you are now. It would be foolhardy on my part to share anything with you, especially since I don't know where your loyalties lie now. You left the marshals almost six years ago. I don't have a sense of who you are."

Brianna waited for Gideon's reaction to that. Callahan had essentially questioned his integrity.

He didn't respond with the anger she might have expected. Instead, he lifted a shoulder in a negligent shrug. "No harm, no foul."

Regret moved into the woman's eyes. "I owe you both an apology," she said slowly. "The truth is, I didn't want to trust you." She divided her gaze between Gideon and Brianna. "I was feeling pretty raw over what happened to Nate and I wanted someone to blame." Her eyes, wide with sincerity, rested on Gideon. "You drew the short straw."

Brianna remained silent as she waited to see Gideon's reaction.

He leaned back in the booth. "I appreciate you reaching out to us. Maybe we can find Jameson and bring him in if we work on it together."

"That would be great. I'm breaking all protocol by meeting you like this, but Nate was a friend. To all of us."

"Yes, he was."

Callahan slid out from the booth and got to her feet. "I'll let you know if and when I learn anything." With a brief nod to both Gideon and Brianna, she and Newhouse left the diner.

"Whew," Brianna said once they were alone. "She made an about-face there."

"She was hard-nosed but fair back before I left the marshals. Looks like she hasn't changed. What did we get from that besides a whole bunch of nothing?"

"I think we got quite a lot. Callahan isn't as casual as she'd have us believe."

"What do you mean?"

"Micro-expressions. They give away a lot. When she asked you about what Nate told you, her lips tightened momentarily before she smoothed them out. And did you notice that she didn't seem particularly upset about Nate until the end?"

Gideon frowned. "Yeah, I picked up on that. He was one of her people."

"Maybe she's not a touchy-feely type person."

"She came to the marshals from the DEA. From what I heard, she had one of the highest performance reviews ever given. She's nobody's fool."

"I didn't say that, only that she seemed cold right up until the end."

"Last I heard, being touchy-feely wasn't a requirement for heading up the regional marshals service. She's a good marshal. As far as I'm concerned, she still is."

Brianna hoped he was right.

It had been a good move to bring Brianna to the meet, Gideon decided. She'd picked up on things he'd missed. It hadn't hurt, either, that she'd evaluated Callahan and Newhouse through a woman's eyes. Women saw things differently than men did, especially when it came to other women.

He was grateful to have her on his side.

He didn't want to admit it, but Nate's death had rocked him to the core. He needed to get himself out of the funk he'd fallen in to. Easier said than done when he'd lost a good friend. That, plus the bullet wound to his arm, had knocked him off his game. Neither were an excuse for his inattention to detail. His and Brianna's lives depended upon his skills and perception being first-rate.

With that in mind, he said, "I want to ditch this phone and get another one." So far he knew of only Callahan and Newhouse who had the number, but that was two people too many.

"Good idea."

They stopped at a convenience store and bought a burner. When he saw a semitruck parked at the side of the store, Gideon put the old phone in its tire well. "Maybe that will slow down anyone who tries to track us down."

"Where to now?" she asked.

He didn't have an answer to that.

He and Brianna needed to go on the offensive. Playing defense had never been his strength—not in football, not in the SEALS, and not now. He'd been trained to take the fight to the enemy.

The only problem was he couldn't identify the enemy. Sure, he knew Jameson, but Jameson was playing it cagey and staying under the radar. Gideon knew he was probably pulling strings from wherever he was holed up, but the trick was finding his hidey-hole.

One thing he knew for certain—the enemy could be anyone. The idea that someone he'd worked with could turn on his colleagues, his friends, left a bad taste in his mouth.

But right now he could trust no one.

TWELVE

The trip back to the motel went smoothly until the truck began to wobble. Gideon brought it to a stop at the side of the road and hopped out.

"Flat tire," he said.

Neither one of them believed it was an accident. Had someone put something in their tire that would slowly deflate it and then followed the truck when they'd had to pull over? Even though they hadn't detected anyone following them, that didn't mean a very skilled operative couldn't have done so.

"Let's get the tire changed and get out of here." He set about changing the tire.

And then she heard it.

The sound of a snapping twig. Only it wasn't a twig. It was the click of a rifle's trigger. She recognized the twang of a metal slide.

"Get down," Gideon ordered. Apparently he'd heard it, too.

Brianna took to the ground immediately.

A bullet whizzed by, with a whiff of air close enough that she could feel it. Though it was well past sundown, a sniper with a scope plus night-vision goggles could pick off a target.

"Don't move," he said.

"Don't worry."

They waited. And waited some more. No more shots, but that didn't mean the shooter was gone. Maybe he was simply biding his time, waiting for her and Gideon to make a stupid move, like getting up and presenting a target.

And then the shots came. From multiple shooters.

The gunfire kept her plastered to the ground, though the bullets didn't come particularly close to her.

Beneath the truck, she saw the feet and legs of one of the attackers. Propping herself up on her elbows, she took aim at the man's ankle.

The bullet hit where she'd sighted her weapon. The ankle was a vulnerable joint.

Crying out, he dropped his weapon and stooped to grab his leg before falling to the ground.

Gideon gave her a thumbs-up.

Her elation died rapidly when she realized that they still had more bad guys to take out.

Gideon was a crack shot and she could hold her own, but five against two was daunting. He must have guessed at her thoughts, for he said,

"Don't worry. We've got this." With that, he took out another man with a bullet to the shoulder. She knew that he didn't want to kill anyone if it could be helped. The men might have information that could help Gideon and the marshals bring in Jameson.

Okay, things were evening up a bit. Brianna checked her weapon, saw that she was down to two rounds.

Gideon held up three fingers.

Five shots to take out four men left little room for error.

"I need to get behind them," he said. "All they have to do is to split up and come at us from both sides and we're cooked."

The picture he painted wasn't a pretty one. She understood too well the implications.

"I don't like leaving you." Worry darkened his eyes.

"Don't worry about me." After the initial shot, which she now believed to be a deliberate miss, the shots had been aimed at Gideon, not at her. "They don't want me dead," she said, reminding him of the theory they'd talked over before. "Do what you have to do. I can take care of myself."

He pressed a quick kiss to her forehead. "I know." With that, he was gone, disappearing into the underbrush.

Brianna touched the spot where Gideon had

kissed her. It had been a fleeting thing, a brush of his lips at most, but it had moved her more than she wanted to admit.

It didn't mean anything, had been the result of an adrenaline-charged moment only, but she couldn't deny the sigh in her heart.

Get your mind off a barely there kiss, she told herself sternly, *and back on to what matters. Staying alive.*

Gideon had operated in all kinds of conditions— the Afghan mountains and desert, the jungles of the Congo and the mean streets of urban meccas.

The thought of four enemy soldiers—and that was how he thought of them—didn't scare him.

What scared him was leaving Brianna alone.

She could handle herself, but a woman was always vulnerable in ways a man was not. What if one of the goons got past him to her?

He set his jaw. It couldn't happen. *Failure is not an option.*

Crawling across the snow-covered ground, cold as it was, he was grateful for the blizzard that was just now blowing in, rendering visibility nil. Cold seeped into him, but he shook it off. He'd been through worse. In fact, one of the first things he'd learned as a SEAL was to get comfortable being uncomfortable.

He spotted one of the men just yards ahead, a

look-out. Foolishly, the man checked his phone, spotlighting his location and making him an easy target. It was a rookie move. Well, that answered one question: he wasn't military or law-enforcement trained. A professional would have known better.

Gideon crept toward his prey. He could have used his weapon, but he didn't want to alert the others, and he wanted to save his ammunition.

When he was within a foot of the man, he reached out and pulled the goon's feet out from under him.

His quarry went down hard.

Gideon followed up with a hard chop to the man's throat, rendering him unconscious. He used the drawstring from the man's hood to bind his hands and feet together and stuffed his glove inside his mouth to prevent him from calling out if he regained consciousness anytime soon.

One down; three to go. Dealing with three tangos was doable.

Staying low, Gideon moved to lower ground, where he could see the three remaining men.

Though they were far from amateurs, they'd made a mistake in clustering together. It made them more vulnerable. They were probably trying to regroup and decide what to do with two of their men already taken out. Or maybe they just thought there was safety in numbers. Either way, it was a mistake.

If Gideon had been the leader of the group, he'd have told the men to fan out and surround their prey, leaving no avenue for escape. A brief smile flickered across his mouth.

They'd just made his job a whole lot easier. Who was he to argue if they wanted to give him a break? His lips curved when he acknowledged that that probably hadn't been their intent at all.

He tossed a rock in their direction, just far enough away that one would have to go investigate. As expected, one man separated from the group to determine where the sound had come from.

Gideon was waiting for him. Silently, he took him out by pressing his thumb and forefinger against the man's neck in a vulnerable spot. When the man slumped over, Gideon dragged him behind a boulder.

Now for the last two.

He approached them from behind. When he was only a few yards away, he said, "Drop your weapons."

As one, the men turned.

"There're two of us, and only one of you," the larger of the two said, self-satisfaction stretching his mouth into a sneer.

"Wrong. There're two of us." Brianna stepped beside Gideon.

He kept his surprise and, yes, his anger to himself. "You heard the lady."

"What makes you think that you two can take us?" the second man demanded. "Way I see it, you've got one man and one wimpy woman to take on two men."

"This." Brianna shot him in the hand. He dropped the weapon and grabbed his hand, howling.

She bent to pick it up; unfortunately, though, she'd inadvertently left herself exposed to the first man. He yanked her up by the hair, then wrapped his arm around her neck and held her in front of him.

"Now you drop your weapon," he ordered Gideon, "or I'll snap her neck. Or maybe I'll just apply a little pressure and she'll be dead that much quicker." He moved one big hand to circle her slender neck.

He was bluffing. Gideon was almost sure of it, but it was that tiny bit of doubt that caused him to hesitate.

"Now," the man said, with an exaggerated drawl, "how 'bout I walk away with the pretty lady in front of me? You stay where you are if you want to see her in one piece again."

"What makes you think I care what happens to her?" That was more than lame, but Gideon was stalling for time. Not by a flicker of his eyes did he let on that the man's words and the sight of his hands around Brianna's neck had gotten to him.

"She's a pretty lady. And if you don't care about her, why were you guarding her?"

The man had him there.

Gideon lifted a shoulder in a careless shrug. "She was a means to an end. Getting to Jameson. That's all I care about. If something happens to her, it's no skin off my nose."

"You're mighty cold."

"Just practical."

"I'm gonna call your bluff," the man said and started moving in the opposite direction, Brianna blocking any shot Gideon might have.

"Not gonna happen. You can walk away from here in bracelets or in a body bag. Your choice."

Gideon dipped his head a fraction of an inch, hoping Brianna picked up on the cue and interpreted it correctly.

She did. In one swift motion she elbowed her captor in the gut and wrenched away from him.

Gideon moved in and threw a fist to the man's jaw, but he didn't go down. Instead, he bared his teeth and moved in.

Gideon delivered a rapid-fire one-two punch to his opponent's midsection. The grunt he heard told him that he'd done some damage.

But was it enough?

Brianna had no time to help Gideon in his fight. Not when the second man, his hand still bleeding from the gunshot wound, charged at her. Lacking much physical strength in her arms, she twisted from the waist and tumbled her foe over her back. He landed hard, but wasn't out; instead, he grabbed her ankle and pulled her down to the ground, where she did a face-plant. She quickly rolled to her back and used her legs to scissor him at the waist.

He wrenched his way free and got to his feet, but she wasn't done with him. Not yet.

She flipped to her feet and struck out with her right leg to kick him in the gut, but he grasped her foot and twisted it, causing her to lose balance and drop to the ground. He was on her before she could defend herself.

"You're gonna pay for that," he said. "Now."

She didn't bother answering. She needed to save her breath for what she was pretty sure would be the fight of her life.

"Cat got your tongue?" he taunted.

So busy was he in mocking her that he failed to notice that she had grabbed a fistful of slush and dirt and clumped it into a ball. Now she smashed it in his face.

He released his hold on her and swiped at his nose and mouth. His hands came away streaked with mud. Hate filled his eyes. "Think you're funny, do you? We'll see how much you feel like laughing when I'm finished with you."

She found nothing funny in the situation and looked wildly about for something else to use as a weapon. She couldn't pull Gideon from his own battle with his opponent. She had only herself to depend upon.

She twisted away from him, but he caught her hair in his good hand and yanked. Hard. She swung her elbow up, catching him in the jaw. A cracking sound told her that the blow may have broken it.

He twisted around, then tossed her to the ground and pressed his knee to her chest, cutting off her air.

She gasped for even the smallest breath. The pressure eased a bit, and she gulped greedily.

"Like that?" he asked. "You're puny enough that I can do that all day. Each time you'll think you're dying. You'll never know when it's going to be the last time."

She didn't believe he'd kill her. Not on purpose, anyway. It was becoming more and more clear that Jameson wanted her alive. But this goon could easily kill her without meaning to.

His smirk grew wider with each moment that he pressed on her chest, his delight in taunting her obvious. Her legs were free and she used them to give her leverage to push him off, but he was too heavy, too strong.

Frantically, she tried to come up with a plan. Then she had it. His ego. She'd use it against him.

She wet her lips with her tongue, trying to work up enough saliva that she could talk. "You think you're the baddest man around, don't you? It'll look real good when my partner lets it out that the only person you could best in a fight was a woman half your size."

"What makes you think your partner's going to be around to let it out?" But she could see the idea troubled him.

"If not him, it's your partner. One way or another, it'll get out. What's going to happen to your rep then?" She put a sneer in her voice. "I can see it now. Your pals snickering at you. Little girls challenging you to a fight."

She knew she was playing with fire. Push him too far and he was likely to kill her out of sheer temper. She had to hit the right note.

"You want to save your rep? Let me go, and we both live to fight another day."

She knew that wasn't going to go over, but she'd managed to stall long enough to get her breath back and wriggled her hands free from where he had clamped them against her hips.

With his knee still on her chest, her foe hadn't realized that her hands were loose. She used them now to reach up and gouge at his eyes.

Surprise and pain distracted him enough to

allow her to push him off her and get to her knees. She pressed her advantage by bringing her elbow down on his neck in a hard chop. While he was recovering, she stumbled to her feet.

Yowling with anger, he sprang up. When he came at her, she was ready and drove her fist into his nose, causing blood to spill down his face.

He swiped at it and, with a roar of rage, charged at her. Between his wounded eyes and temper, he missed her by a good six inches. Hardly a great distance, but big enough when it came to hand-to-hand combat.

She stuck out her foot, tripping him. This time when he fell, he hit his head on a rock and was knocked out momentarily. She held him in place with a foot at the base of his neck. "Stay down if you know what's good for you."

The man twisted beneath her foot, but she didn't let up the pressure.

"You won't get off so easy next time," he said between clenched teeth.

"If I have my way, there won't be a next time," she retorted.

Gideon finished off his man with a blow to the jaw, which sent him sprawling. He kneeled and bound the man's hands with flex-cuffs, then passed a set to Brianna.

With their hands cuffed, it was easy enough to bind their feet.

"That should hold them," she said.

"Why did they come after us that way rather than just shooting us?" she asked Gideon. Then, hunkering down, she shook the man she'd fought. "What did you want to know? Why didn't you try to kill us?"

"Orders."

That, she could believe. But whose orders? "Who gave them?"

"That's for me to know and you to find out." The smart-mouth answer did nothing to defuse her temper.

She squeezed his injured hand and pressed her thumb and forefinger to a vulnerable spot on the man's neck. Such a hold could kill if she moved her finger a fraction of an inch. Apparently the man knew that. His eyes widened while his breathing grew shallow. "No way you'll kill me."

"Is that so?"

"Yeah." But he didn't sound so certain this time. He was right, but Brianna wasn't about to tell him so.

She increased the pressure just enough to make him wonder.

The man bucked, but she didn't give him room to maneuver. "I don't know who's giving the orders. I don't report to whoever's in charge. And that's the truth. Asking questions gets you killed, so I keep my mouth shut and do what I'm told."

She pressed the man further in an attempt to wring any other information she could from him, but either the man was a first-class actor or he honestly didn't know anything more.

"Whadda you gonna do to me?"

"That's for me to know and you to find out," she said, throwing the man's words back at him.

He muttered something under his breath that Brianna couldn't catch. She figured she was better off not knowing.

"What are we going to do with them?" she asked Gideon out of earshot of their prisoners.

"I'll make a call to S and J, give them the location," Gideon said. "Someone there will call the police and have our six friends here picked up." He looked about. "I want to put a whole lot of gone between us and the police when they show up. We don't know who we can trust, and I don't feel like playing 'guess the mole.'"

"I'm with you. We've been here too long as it is."

"I know. If these six clowns don't return within a reasonable time, Jameson's likely to send out others looking for them. They might be smarter than these goons."

The last thing she wanted was for her and Gideon to confront another team of hitters.

THIRTEEN

The danger was over. For now.

Gideon was grateful Brianna wasn't hurt, but he was angry she'd put herself in harm's way. Didn't she realize that his every decision, every move, was designed to protect her?

"I thought I told you to stay put." He held his shoulders rigid, afraid if he let them relax by so much as a fraction of an inch, his hold on his anger would disappear as well. He wanted…no, he needed to hold on to it.

"You did. But I got worried when you didn't return right away."

"There were four men to take out," he reminded her.

She fisted her hands on her hips and raised her chin. "I know. That's why I was worried. I apologize if I scared you, but I won't apologize for worrying about you." She took a breath. Another. Giving herself time, he thought, to gather her outrage. "So live with it."

The snap in her voice sparked his temper.

"You almost got yourself killed!" The fury he'd tamped down only moments ago now burst through. "Don't you get it? You almost died. If that goon had been a little bit faster or you'd been a little bit slower, you'd be dead."

What if something had happened to her on his watch? He couldn't have lived with it, couldn't have lived with himself. Didn't she get it?

The mutinous look on her face said no.

Gideon called S&J and asked his second-in-command to call the cops and explain things. Jameson was said to have friends in the police department, and Gideon didn't want to stick around in case one of those *friends* happened to show up.

Tension filled the truck on the return trip.

"I'm sorry for coming down on you like that," he said at last. When he'd regained his calm, he knew he'd been unfair.

"No problem."

But there was. He could see it in the set of her shoulders and hear it in the clipped words.

"I was trying to keep you safe." Why couldn't she understand that? Righteous anger began to fill him once again.

She didn't respond, proving to him that she had been at fault. Immediately, the ridiculousness of that thought shamed him. There was no *fault*, no blame to cast. She'd been trying to protect him just as he'd been trying to protect her.

Her next words gave proof to it. "And I was trying to do the same for you. What makes it right on your part and not on mine?"

The reasonableness of the question should have alerted him to stay quiet, but reason was not in his wheelhouse, not when Brianna had almost been killed. He settled on the only thing he could say. "Because you're the client."

She snorted at that.

Gideon was still stewing over the idea of a mole in the US Marshals Service. He knew that good people could turn, but he didn't like thinking someone he knew and had worked with could have betrayed his friends. Someone in the federal law-enforcement system wanting more power and more money. The list of suspects was endless.

They needed someone to have their backs. Michael "Chap" Chapman, ex-Marshal and now an S&J operative, came to mind.

"I'm calling Michael Chapman," he told Brianna. "I recruited him to work at S and J. Someone else needs to know what's going on. In case…"

He didn't finish. He figured he didn't need to.

"Chap's a good guy," she said without commenting on the unfinished sentence.

"Yeah. He's going through a bad time, lost his fiancée a few months ago, but he'll come through if we need him."

He made the call, told him the little they knew, and, with a "Thanks, man," hung up. "Okay," he said to Brianna. "Chap knows what's going on. If we need help, he'll be here."

After breakfast the following morning, they headed to the truck, where they found a note attached to the windshield. The printing was messy but legible, with an address and instructions for Gideon to come alone if he wanted to find Jameson. The words *come alone* were underlined.

"Someone's found us," he said. "Get your stuff. We won't be coming back here."

He texted the address to Chap and asked that he check it out.

"It's a setup," Brianna said flatly.

"Yeah. But what choice do I have? If we want information, I have to risk it." He needed to put an end to this. If it meant walking into a trap, he'd do it.

"You mean *we* have to risk it."

"No way. You're not going. I won't risk you."

She planted her hands on her hips.

"The instructions said for me to come alone," he pointed out.

"You're not going alone, and I'm not staying

behind. The only way this works out is that we go together. Or we don't go at all."

Gideon knew when he was beaten. "Okay. Let's do it."

The abandoned factory, with its forlorn-looking parking lot, was mute evidence of hard times. Broken windows with jagged edges appeared as giant maws ready to swallow the unwary.

Brianna had had a bad feeling about this from the beginning. The fact that someone had found them to slip the piece of paper on the truck's windshield bothered her more than a little. They hadn't talked about how they'd been found, but she knew it was weighing on Gideon, just as it was on her.

"This screams setup," she said once more.

"I know, but if there's something to help us find Jameson, I have to do it." He had already climbed out of the truck and started toward the building, his long strides eating up the distance. "Stay in the truck," he called over his shoulder.

She scrambled out. "You go, I go. I know you want to find whoever murdered Nate as well as find Jameson, but this isn't the way," she said once she'd caught up with him.

He reached the front door, tested it and found it unlocked. "I'm just going to look around for a minute."

The interior of the building was what you'd expect. Empty. Musty-smelling. A stack of pallets leaned against the far wall. A flight of stairs extended up to a loft with another going down.

After five minutes without anyone showing up, she hoped Gideon was ready to call it quits.

When his phone rang, he checked the number. "Chap." He put it on speaker. "What do you have for me?"

"Not much. The building is owned by a shell company. No name or address given."

Frustration leaked through Gideon's voice. "There must be a name somewhere."

"That's a big fat zero."

Chap supplied a few more details, but Brianna wasn't really listening as her internal alarm ratcheted up with every passing minute. The hair on the back of her neck rose. Her skin prickled, and her heart picked up its beat until she was certain it would burst out of her chest.

The certainty that something was very wrong pinged every sense. The smart thing was to get out of here as quickly as possible. She only hoped it wasn't already too late. Just as she was about to tell Gideon that they needed to beat a hasty retreat, the world exploded.

As debris rained down on them, Gideon pulled Brianna to him and pushed her down, then did his best to cover her, protecting her with his own body.

Wave after wave of explosions rocked the building. Even after the deafening noise ended, the building seemed to shudder and the sound reverberated through him.

Before he could react to it, the floor gave way, and they fell through.

When they landed a good ten feet below, he moved his right arm experimentally. Okay. Nothing broken there. He did the same with his left arm, then his right leg. But when he tested his left leg, he knew he was in trouble.

It refused to move.

In fact, the whole leg seemed pinned to the floor.

Something wet dripped into his left eye. He reached up to wipe it away, then looked at his blood-streaked hand, but didn't grow alarmed. Head wounds tended to bleed profusely.

More concerning was the pain that speared through his leg. He did his best to ignore it.

But the red mist of agony already overtaking him wouldn't be ignored.

He pushed himself up and saw what was causing dozens of misery-tipped arrows to pierce his leg. A piece of rebar was sticking out of his leg, right above the knee.

He must have blacked out for a minute, or

maybe two, because when he regained consciousness, he couldn't remember where he was or what had happened.

Then he remembered. The explosion. The building falling down on them. Did that really happen? He looked at his leg again.

Yeah. It happened.

Once more, he closed his eyes for a moment. Or a lot of moments. The next thing he knew someone was talking at him. Not talking to him because he wasn't talking back. At least, he didn't think he was. He wasn't sure, and that frightened him more than anything.

The voice grew more insistent. "Gideon. Can you hear me?"

He forced an eye open. "Wh-what?" The other eye followed suit. He saw Brianna. She looked worse for wear, with her face covered in concrete dust, her hair a mess of wild curls and a gash on her shoulder. "You're bleeding."

"It's nothing."

Nothing looked like something, as blood stained her shirt and more seeped from the wound on her shoulder.

"Do you remember what happened?" she asked.

Why was she shouting at him? Didn't she know that he hurt all over? Except for his ears. They were the only thing that didn't hurt. He felt compelled to point that out. "My ears are working just fine."

She pointed to the metal bar sticking out of his leg. "Glad to hear it," she said in a lower voice. "We need to get this thing out of you."

His thinking was still a bit slow, but he knew that was going to hurt. "Maybe we ought to leave it in. Until, you know, we get some help."

"We don't know how long that'll be. In the meantime, sepsis could set in. And in these conditions..." Her hands made an expressive gesture, one that even his muzzy brain could interpret.

"Not good," he said in an understatement to top all understatements.

"No. Not good at all."

"You're going to pull it out?" he asked.

"Yeah. But first, we need to find something to patch you up after we get it out." She looked around the basement. "The pickings are slim, but I see a couple of things."

"Like what? Never mind," he said on second thought. "Don't tell me."

She left him and, after picking her way through narrow canyons formed by fallen support beams, rubble and chunks of concrete, returned carrying a bottle of bleach and a dusty roll of duct tape.

"That the best you could do?"

"Sorry." And she sounded like she was. "I'm

not going to lie to you. This is going to hurt. A lot."

Her eyes filled with tears, and, for the first time since he'd regained consciousness, he thought about something, someone, beside himself. He'd been a Navy SEAL. He could handle whatever was thrown at him.

He did his best to pull a grin out from somewhere, wanting to reassure her. "Gotcha."

"It's okay if you want to yell. Or cry. Or pass out. That'd probably be best." The tears streamed down her face, creating rivulets in the concrete dust.

He reached up, wanting to brush them away. "You're really making me look forward to this." Dread crawled through him even as he accepted that it had to be done.

She caught his hand and pressed it to her lips, then ripped the good sleeve from her shirt and doubled it over. After repeating the process several times, she handed it to him. "Bite down on this."

"How am I supposed to do that and scream at the same time?" A joke. If he was still capable of making jokes, things couldn't be too bad.

"You'll figure it out."

After wrapping her hands around the rebar, she pulled it from his leg. Before he could react to that particular agony, she poured bleach on the

wound—another torture to his battered body—
and then quickly covered it with duct tape.

Pain such as he'd never known screamed
through him just before blackness overcame him.

What do you know? He was going to pass out
after all.

FOURTEEN

Brianna didn't cry often. She'd cried when Jack had died but had put the tears behind her when she'd learned she was carrying his baby. She hadn't cried when she'd had to uproot Ruthie from her home. Not after the first time, anyway. She hadn't cried when she'd learned that Jameson was out. She hadn't cried when she'd had to leave Ruthie. At least, not much.

But she cried now.

Great, gulping sobs that caused her entire body to shake. These were not the pretty tears that you saw actresses on television or the movies indulge in, tears that glistened like diamonds and didn't ruin one iota of their carefully applied makeup.

No, these were messy tears that smeared over her dirt-stained face in a goopy mixture of salt and concrete dust. These were real tears from deep down inside, where grief and pain and the occasional spark of joy resided. These were tears that wouldn't come to a halt with a good pep talk.

She'd inflicted unspeakable pain upon Gideon. If she could, she would have taken it herself rather than do that to him, but such things weren't possible.

This went beyond simple human compassion and straight to the core of her feelings for him. Though she wanted to deny it, she was falling in love with him.

The question of what else she could have done to save him tormented her until she wanted to clap her hands over her ears to block the taunting words that resounded in her mind.

Suck it up, girl. You're not out of this yet.

She did her best to wipe her face with the tail of her shirt, but soon gave it up as a lost cause.

A favorite line of scripture came to mind and brought a measure of comfort. *The righteous is delivered out of trouble, and the wicked cometh in his stead.*

She let the words settle in her heart. Calmer now, she began to assess the situation.

Gideon hadn't regained consciousness yet. She counted it as a blessing, knowing he'd probably awake to agony. Better to prolong that for as long as possible.

What if the wound developed sepsis despite her precautions? She pushed away that thought. She couldn't go there. Not now, when there was nothing she could do about it.

There'd be time enough for second-guessing herself later if she had to. For the moment, though, she had to get past that and decide what to do next.

Their situation, however, namely being trapped in a basement with an entire four-thousand-square-foot building on top of them, couldn't be ignored forever.

If only she could get a cell signal. She'd tried in different locations in the basement and hadn't been able to bring up a single bar. So much for her provider's guarantee that she'd have a signal anywhere.

When Gideon stirred, she gave his arm a gentle squeeze. "It's all right." Had she ever told a bigger lie?

She watched as his body went rigid in an attempt to contain the pain that must be throbbing through him. The lines on his face deepened with every breath.

"I thought maybe I'd died and this was heaven."

Despite their circumstances, and they were beyond grim, she managed a lopsided smile. "Sorry. We're still on earth." That bit of humor aside, she was feeling pretty beat-up herself, and despite her best efforts to keep the hated tears at bay, they started to fall again. They fell because as bad as Gideon must feel, he'd tried to lighten her burden.

He was a hero in every way, and she couldn't help feeling that she was letting him down with her tears. He needed her strength right now, not her weakness.

"I'm sorry," she said, gulping back the unwanted tears.

"Hey, you have a right to cry. You just performed field surgery on me and didn't balk once." He touched her cheek.

"So why am I falling apart now?"

"Because the stress is over."

She made a point of looking around. "Really? We're stuck in a basement of a building that was blown up and could collapse the rest of the way on us at any moment. You're injured. And I'm a mess." She sniffled. And sniffled again. "And I can't stop crying."

"Well, some of the stress is over," he said. "Take four deep breaths, slowly in and out."

"What's that supposed to do?" She didn't even try to keep the resentment out of her voice.

"It's called combat breathing. It'll help calm you down. A buddy on the team taught it to me."

She did as he said and felt better. "Thanks."

He turned his head and looked around. "Nothing but the finest accommodations, I see."

"Only the best."

"Thank you." The lighthearted banter had left his voice. "You saved my life."

"I don't know about that. I pulled a piece of rebar from your leg, poured bleach over it and then wrapped duct tape around your wound. If you don't have a raging infection, it's not because I didn't do my best to give you one. Last I knew, none of what I did was in *Gray's Anatomy*."

"You saved my life," he repeated. "If not for you, I could have—probably would have—bled out. So, thank you."

Uncomfortable with the praise, she stuffed the threatening tears down deep and focused on what they had to do to get out of here, but she had nothing. "We're trapped in here."

"Yeah. I got that."

"I've tried getting a cell signal, but it was a nonstarter. What we need right now is a brilliant plan."

He grabbed the piece of rebar she'd pulled from his leg and propped himself up to a sitting position. Then he started banging it against a pipe.

"Good rhythm," she said, "but the melody could use some work." But she knew what he was doing—trying to alert the people who must be looking for survivors of the explosion.

She found another piece of metal and did the same. "When we get out of here, how about we start a band?"

"Sounds good. I get to play drums, though. You can lay down the riff on a guitar."

After five minutes of continuous banging against the pipe, he lied back, exhaustion and pain etched on his face. "We'll start again in a minute or two."

"Sure." She put down her makeshift drumstick as well. If Gideon needed to rest, then that's what they'd do. No rush. The only problem was that the oxygen wouldn't last forever down here. Without oxygen, they would die. It was as simple as that. Another concern reared its head. What if the explosion had caused a gas leak? What then?

She and Gideon wouldn't know it until it was too late.

Gideon's eyes were closed, and hers were about to, when she heard a banging. Or she thought she'd heard it.

She sat up.

Listened.

There it was again.

She picked up her piece of metal and banged against the pipe with all her might. An answering clank told her that she hadn't imagined it after all.

"Gideon. Gideon. Wake up. They've found us."

Gideon looked up, his gaze suddenly sharp. "Shh. It's Morse code."

She didn't bother asking if he was certain. He was former military, after all.

"What's it saying?"

"Shh."

She didn't much like being shushed, but she kept quiet.

He listened some more. "They want us to move to the southeast corner of the basement. Seems there's a vent shaft there that they can send down a harness."

Hope, that precious commodity, filled her. Then she looked at the obstacles they had to go around, under, or over to get to the opposite corner of the building. It was only forty yards, but it might as well have been forty miles.

"We can do it," he said, apparently guessing her thoughts. He sounded more like his old self. At another series of taps, he held up his hand, head cocked as he listened some more.

"Of course," she said, though what she wanted to do was break down and bawl like a baby. How were they supposed to cover forty yards in the shape they were in and not disturb anything? Gideon could barely move at all. "We wouldn't want that."

He flashed her a confident smile. "We got this."

With painstaking care, they picked their way toward the southeast corner, avoiding wires that gave off sparks dangling from the ceiling and stepping over hunks of concrete. Their progress was good until they encountered a large beam that blocked the way. Going over it wasn't an option.

"We need something we can use as a lever," Gideon said.

She looked around and spied a narrow but sturdy-looking pipe. With infinite care, she pulled it from a pile of debris. "How's this?"

"Perfect."

He fit the pipe beneath the beam, and, with more strength than she thought he had, given what he'd been through, he pressed on it and lifted the beam a foot off the ground before letting it down.

"This'll work. When I give you the signal, slide underneath," he said. "I won't be able to hold it for long."

"What about you?"

He lowered his gaze. "Let's get you through first."

And then she got it. He was giving her the opportunity to live while he stayed behind. Possibly to die.

"We go together or we don't go at all," she said, acutely conscious that she'd said those same words earlier. "No compromise on this." Not on Gideon's life.

"You have a daughter who needs you."

"All the more reason that we get out of here. Both of us." She'd thought it through. "What if I slide beneath the beam, get on the other side of it and you throw the lever over? Then I'll use it to lift from the other side?"

"It's going to take everything I have to lift this. How are you going to do it?"

"I'll manage." She stared at him with a look that said she wasn't going to back down. "What other choice do we have?"

"Get ready." He lifted the beam one more time, and she rolled beneath.

"You okay?" he called.

"Yeah. Toss the pipe over."

He threw it.

"My turn now," she said and picked up the pipe. She pressed down on it with everything she had.

And prayed. With everything she had.

Nothing.

Again.

Did it move? She brought her whole weight down on it, making her wish she'd had a few more slices of pizza the other night.

"It's moving," she yelled.

Thirty seconds later, Gideon had rolled out beneath the beam. "How you did that, I'll never know."

"I had some help."

Confusion crossed his face, and then he nodded. "Help from above."

"That's right. With the Lord on my side, I knew I could do it."

Gideon didn't weigh in on that.

They made their way to the corner, where he tapped out a message. Tapping from the outside ensued.

"They're sending down a harness," he said.

When it arrived, he started to help her into it.

She shook her head. "No way. You're the one who's injured. You go first."

"Not gonna happen."

"When you were on deployment and one of your men was hurt, who did you make sure was rescued first?"

"That's different."

She stood firm. "Are we going to stand here arguing or are you going to get your butt in that sling so we can both get out of here?"

"Anyone ever tell you that you're one stubborn lady?" he asked, frustration, along with admiration, eking through.

"No one but you," she said sweetly and proceeded to help him into the harness.

It took some doing, the harness being designed for a smaller individual, but they managed. After he was pulled to the top, the harness was then sent back down for Brianna.

When she got to the top, she grinned at him. "We did it."

"Yeah, but the bad guys almost won," he said, his voice filled with hard resolve. "Now it's time for payback."

FIFTEEN

Gideon gulped in huge breaths of air. Nothing had ever tasted as sweet. He attempted to wave off the EMT who hovered over him.

"Sir, we need to get you to the hospital."

"I'm fine…" He wasn't, but he couldn't spare the time to go to the hospital. He had to find the people who had set them up.

"Begging your pardon, sir, but you don't look fine. You look like you just had a building fall on you."

"If he gives you any problems, let me know. I'll make sure he toes the line." It was Michael Chapman. He turned his attention to Gideon. "Good thing I knew where you were."

Gideon knew his friend had probably been pushing the rescue effort. "Thanks, man."

"Nothing you wouldn't have done for me." The steady look that passed between them said more than words could.

Gideon looked down at the duct tape wrapped

around his leg. Maybe the EMT had a point. He pointed to Brianna. "Make sure you see to her, too."

"Yes, sir. Now let's get you to the hospital."

"Okay." He submitted to being strapped on a gurney and placed in an ambulance. Still, he felt the urge to make a joke. "I've done worse shaving."

"Yes, sir."

In the ambulance, an IV was placed in one arm, pumping him with antibiotics and fluids, while a blood-pressure cuff was attached to the other. Hands prodded and poked, but he was too weary to object.

After a blur of a trip, he was taken to the ER.

"Whoever treated you saved your life," a young doctor said after a look at Gideon's leg. "He'd have done MacGyver proud."

"She," Gideon mumbled. "It was a she." A laugh rumbled out as he recalled the TV hero who could make something out of nothing. "And she would at that."

"I'm going to give you something to put you to sleep. When you wake up, you'll feel a whole lot better."

Gideon didn't object. A little rest sounded good right about now.

"Looks like you've had a bullet wound treated

recently. Let me guess. The same lady took it out."

"Yeah."

"We'll check that out, but it looks like the wound is healing nicely. That is one gutsy lady to do what she did."

"The gutsiest." Gideon was fading. His tongue felt thick and refused to do what he ordered it to. With a sigh, he gave in to sleep.

When he awoke several hours later, he decided he'd live. Though the pain that had clawed through him earlier had stilled, stiffness barked through his leg as he tried to lift it a few inches off the bed.

Well, what did he expect? He'd endured a pretty substantial injury. It would have been worse, far worse, without Brianna treating it as she had. What a woman.

Maybe she'd shed some tears, but she'd stepped up and had done what was necessary. He'd known battle-hardened soldiers who would have balked at treating an injury such as his.

The expression on her face had been resolute. She hadn't screamed or backed away in horror, had only quietly set about doing the unthinkable.

He owed her. Especially since it had been his fault that they'd ended up in that predicament.

Sure, he'd wanted information on Rex Jameson's whereabouts, but that wasn't the real reason he'd walked into what was most likely a trap. He'd wanted to find the person who had killed Nate and had figured that was the best way to do it.

If he'd listened to Brianna, they could have avoided the whole thing. As it was, they'd barely survived and still had no clue as to where Jameson was and if it had been him or someone else who had murdered his friend.

No doubt about it, Gideon decided. He'd messed up. Big-time.

After being treated in the emergency room, Brianna had one more pressing stop to make at the hospital.

At the explosion site she'd done her best to avoid the EMTs, but the earnest-faced young man hovering over her hadn't been having it.

You've got a nasty-looking head wound, ma'am, he'd said.

Ma'am. When did she get to be a *ma'am*? Okay, she did have a five-year-old child, but he didn't know that.

She'd wanted to tell him that she wasn't a *ma'am* but had saved her breath. It hadn't mattered. All that mattered was finding out how badly Gideon had been injured. The only reason she'd given in to the hospital trip was to see him.

Now, stitched up, full of antibiotics to ward

off infection and feeling considerably better, she found Gideon in a recovery room.

"You look like you had a building fall on you," he said.

"And you look like you just stepped out of *GQ*."

"Actually, you're beautiful."

Self-consciously, she touched the abrasions on her face, then her hair, which was still covered with cement dust and who-knew-what-else. "I look a fright. You were right the first time."

"No. I owe you my life."

"It was a joint effort. The important thing is that we came through it."

"Right."

"When you get out of here in a couple of days—"

"Wait a minute. Who said anything about a couple of days?"

"I just figured—"

"You figured wrong. One day will fix me up just fine."

She wasn't going to win an argument with him and gave in, albeit ungracefully. "All right. When you get out of here and rest up—" The look on his face had her walking back the last words. "When you get out of here, we go after whoever set us up."

"That's better." A minute, maybe more, of silence stretched between them. "I owe you a big apology."

"For what?"

"For nearly getting us killed. If I'd listened to you—"

Brianna was shaking her head. "You did what you felt you had to. I was the one who insisted on going along. You tried to stop me."

"You ended up saving my life. If it hadn't been for you, I'd still be buried under thousands of pounds of concrete."

"We saved each other. You put your life on the line for Ruthie and me over and over. Pulling you out of that basement was the least I could do." She'd kept her words deliberately light, but she meant every one of them.

She could never repay him for saving her daughter.

Never.

She didn't say the rest, that she'd do anything to save him. Her feelings for him were growing with every day.

Her heart longed to tell him of what was inside, but she couldn't. She didn't have the courage.

Gideon awoke the following morning sore, bruised and impatient.

He argued with the nurse, argued with the doctor and only succeeded in having them throw up their hands and stalk off.

When Brianna showed up, he scowled at her. "They—" he jerked his thumb in the direction of the doorway "—don't want to release me."

She gave him a critical look. "Could it be because you just had your leg stitched up? I heard it took over two dozen stitches to sew it back together."

"I've done worse shaving."

"So you told me and anyone else who would listen."

"Okay. So maybe it was a few more."

The concession cost him, and he swallowed down his embarrassment at making it.

"Give it a few more hours," she suggested. "I brought you something for breakfast."

His stomach rumbled. The oatmeal and fruit the hospital served for breakfast was pitifully inadequate.

He looked inside the bag and found two bacon sandwiches. "How did you know this was just what I needed?" He didn't wait for an answer as he started eating.

"I wish it was more," she said, "but I didn't want to go out."

To his shame, he realized he hadn't thought about her safety or where she'd spent last night. "Where did you sleep last night?"

"An orderly set up a cot for me in your room. By the way, you snore."

A confusing mix of feelings filled him, but he didn't give voice to them. Instead, he focused on the last sentence. "Do not."

"Have it your way."

He grinned. The banter felt almost as good as the food tasted.

When he finished the first, he started to open the second sandwich before realizing that she had probably brought it for herself. He pushed it toward her. "Sorry."

"Don't be. That's for you. I figured you'd need it."

"You figured right." The grin he felt tugging at his lips at their byplay disappeared abruptly. "I need to get out of here. For one thing, whoever set us up has to know where I am by now. I don't want to make myself a sitting duck."

"I'll see what I can do."

Forty-five minutes later, Brianna returned. "I have good news and bad news. The good news is that you can be released today. The bad news is that you'll do it against doctor's orders."

"Thanks for springing me."

She handed him a plastic bag. "New clothes. Well, almost new. The ones you were wearing were shredded. The hospital has clothes on hand for indigent patients."

She'd brought him clothes? The gesture moved him more than he could say. "Uh…" He cleared his throat. "Thanks. Again."

"You're welcome. I'll clear out so you can get dressed."

In the bag, he found everything he needed, including a razor and other toiletries, plus a large roll of duct tape, which caused him to grin. Dressed in the new clothes, right down to new shoes and socks, he opened the door and found her in the hallway.

"Let's get out of here," he said.

Gideon didn't believe in revenge. It was wasted effort and time. But he did believe in justice. Right now he wanted justice for Nate and the judge and the others whom Jameson had killed.

The question was, who had set them up? He had little doubt that the same person who had killed Nate had tried to do the same to him.

He'd find whoever had done it. He owed Nate that.

SIXTEEN

Brianna set her teeth. "I'm getting tired of being followed." They'd picked up a tail shortly after leaving the hospital. Obviously someone had been assigned to watch them and signal a partner when they left.

"What's your plan?"

Brianna knew the area, knew that the road dead-ended in a short distance. Construction had been started to make a bypass from the highway to another major artery, but had been halted due to lack of funds.

When they reached the end of the road, she did a three-point turn and started back the way she'd come.

As predicted, their tail was barreling down the road, then came to an abrupt stop when the driver saw their pickup heading toward him.

"Let's see what they've got," she said. Now she was the aggressor.

"Yeah." His voice was remarkably calm given that they were headed straight toward the truck.

The driver switched to Reverse and was backing down the road as fast as he could. Meanwhile, the passenger was leaning out the window and firing at Gideon and Brianna.

"Can you shoot?" she asked, knowing his arm was still sore.

"Let's find out." He fired off three shots in rapid succession. Two struck the engine, the third hitting the windshield.

The sedan sputtered to a stop.

Brianna and Gideon jumped out of the truck and ran toward the car before the men had time to recover.

Gideon yanked open the driver's side door and pulled the driver from the car. "Hand me your weapon and get down on the ground."

Brianna did the same with the man on the passenger side.

"Did Jameson send you?" Gideon demanded.

Both men refused to answer.

Gideon pulled the roll of duct tape from his jacket pocket. "Let's tie 'em up. They can wait for the police right here and explain to them how they came to be working for Jameson."

"Hey, it's freezing out here," the driver objected. He was right. A hard wind funneled down the narrow street, blasting them all with frigid air.

"You'll be warm enough until the boys in blue get here." She secured both men's hands and feet while Gideon held his weapon on them. "They won't be going anywhere."

"Do you mind if I drive this time?" he asked.

She tossed him the keys. "If you think you're up to it."

"I'm definitely up to it. I don't think my blood pressure can take another ride with you."

"What's the matter? Is your blood pressure a sissy?"

"No. But it needs time to settle before I get in a car with you behind the wheel again."

For the first time in hours, she gave a genuine smile. "I'll take that as a compliment." Another vehicle pulled up. Though the goons who climbed out were big and brawny, she felt confident that she and Gideon could handle them, and then she remembered that he had sustained two serious injuries.

"We're not going to get out of here without a fight," Gideon said.

They squared off with the two opponents. Hers easily topped six feet. He moved like a boxer, was light on his feet and snuck in quick hard-hitting punches.

She checked on Gideon, and saw that he was holding his own against his opponent.

That moment of inattention cost her, and her

foe punched her in the jaw and sent her sprawling. Before she could get up, the man straddled her and clipped her at the side of her neck.

Gideon fought off his man, throwing him to the ground, and got to Brianna. He yanked the coward off her. "You wanna try that with me?"

She sprang up, ready to square off with her opponent once more, until a man climbed out of the back seat of one of the vehicles. Though he'd changed over the six years, had shaved his head, recognition set in immediately. Dread caused her to miss a step, allowing her foe to get in a punch to the side of her head.

Rex Jameson.

The man behind everything.

He motioned for two of his men to hold Gideon by the arms. "Good to see you, Stratham. And you." His gaze roamed over Brianna. "I hear you changed your name. Brianna. I like it. It suits you better than Leah."

How had he known she'd changed her name? One of his goons could have found out and told him. Or had he learned it from someone else?

"What? Aren't the two of you going to greet your old pal? What do you say, Stratham?" He spat out the word like an expletive, then wiped a hand over his lips, as though to wipe away the taste of it.

"We were never pals," Gideon said.

"No. We weren't," Jameson agreed, eyes glittering with temper. "I remember how you testified against me. You did your best to ruin my life. I spent six years, six long years, in that prison, planning on how to pay you back." He turned his attention to Brianna. "How's it going, sweet thing?" he asked and ran his hand down her cheek.

Revulsion shuddered through her.

"You don't have to play like you don't like me. I could tell you had a thing for me in the courtroom."

Since that was totally absurd, she didn't bother responding.

Apparently Jameson picked up on her antipathy toward him, because he scowled. "Too good for the likes of me, are you?" He pushed her away in disgust. When she stumbled and fell to the ground, wet with slush and mud, he sneered. "Got your hands dirty, did you? They'll get a lot more dirty before I'm finished with you."

Over the years, Gideon had endured his share of pain and then some. Seeing Jameson put his hands on Brianna was more than he could bear, though, and he wrenched away from the two men who held him and smashed his fist into Jameson's mouth.

Jameson spat out blood, then motioned the

men to take Gideon by the arms once more. "You think that bothers me?"

Standing at six-four, and what was probably around two hundred and fifty pounds, Jameson had a couple of inches and at least sixty pounds on Gideon. He drew back his fist and then slammed it into Gideon's jaw.

Brianna started toward Gideon, but another man seized hold of her. Gideon wanted to tell her to stop struggling, that it was futile, and to save her energy, but he couldn't move his mouth enough to get the words out.

"I can't tell you how long I've waited for this," Jameson said with another slug to Gideon's face. At a signal from him, the men released Gideon and stepped away. Jameson then wrapped his huge hands around Gideon's neck and squeezed.

Can't breathe.

Without oxygen, the brain starts to shut down, but Gideon dug deep and found one last burst of effort. He grabbed Jameson's forearms and yanked them from his neck, breaking his hold, but his strength was waning.

The big man wasn't finished.

He clapped his huge hands against either side of Gideon's head, causing him to reel, his ears ringing. He knew he was losing the battle. A head butt had him seeing double. Dizzy, he couldn't get his bearings.

One more shot and he slumped to the ground.

He thought he heard Brianna call out his name, but he was fading quickly. A moment later, he gave in to the beckoning blackness.

Brianna and Gideon were tossed in the back of a covered truck. Worried about him, she found it hard to focus on anything else. The drive could have lasted ten minutes, twenty, thirty—she couldn't tell.

Gideon hadn't stirred, and she feared he'd suffered a concussion or some kind of brain injury. Shouldn't he have woken by now? All she could do was to cradle his head in her lap.

"We're going to get through this," she murmured to him and reached for his hand.

Did he squeeze her hand in return? She held on to the hope that he had been only temporarily knocked out, and prepared for what was to come.

She did her best to memorize the route the van took. Two left turns before settling in to a steady speed on what must have been a paved highway.

When the van stopped and the door was opened, she was ready. With all the strength she could muster in the enclosed space, she kicked out and caught one of the men in the chest.

The ensuing grunt of pain told her she'd caused some damage.

"You didn't tell me she was dangerous," a voice grumbled.

"I told you she'd been a US Marshal. That should have been enough." That from Jameson. "Get her out."

She was hauled none too gently from the van and thrown to the ground. Gideon was given the same treatment.

Jameson yanked her by the arm. "Get up. We've got business." He marched her into a metal building.

The structure appeared to be some kind of bunker, designed for a doomsday prepper. Single rooms, with doors replaced with bars, lined the lower floor. She assumed they were supposed to be bedrooms, but now they took on the appearance of cells. Since Gideon had been carried away, he'd probably been tossed in one of those cells.

Brianna glared at Jameson, not caring that he saw the repugnance in her gaze. "You haven't changed. You always were a coward."

He slapped her with the back of his hand.

She barely remained on her feet, but she refused to cower before him. Men like Jameson fed on the fear of others. "Why don't you do it again? Or don't you feel man enough to hit a woman a second time?"

"You always did have a mouth on you. Too bad

it's going to cost you. But not before I get what I want from you."

"What are you talking about?"

"You and that husband of yours stole from me and then set me up to take the fall with my people."

She had no idea what he was talking about and said so.

"Don't play innocent with me. You'll tell me what I want to know soon enough."

"You're talking in riddles. I don't have anything of yours. I never did." She rubbed her hands together as though to wipe away filth.

"No?" The taunt in his voice promised retribution. "We'll see about that."

"Is this thing you think I have why you sent your men after us?"

He gave her a what-do-you-think? look.

"You could have killed us. Killed my—" She broke off.

"Your daughter," he said, finishing for her. "Yes, I know about her. If I'd gotten my hands on her, you'd talk. But we'll see how you do when we start beating on your boyfriend again. That little show was just the warm-up act."

With a flick of his hand, he ordered two of his men to take her away.

Once they left her in a cell, she began to pray. And as she did, a much-loved scripture settled in her heart: *I will never leave thee, nor forsake thee.*

A sweet peace washed over her. The Lord was there with her, as He had been throughout her life, even when she'd felt unbearably alone. She had only to hold on to Him.

Please tell me what to do, she pleaded silently. *Gideon and I are in trouble and need Your help. I have to get back to Ruthie. I can't leave her alone.*

She ended the prayer and started thinking like the trained marshal she'd been.

One of the first elements of escape was to assess your surroundings, and she looked about, evaluating if there was anything in the tiny cell that she could turn into a weapon. What did she have to work with? She didn't see anything but a cot and a bucket.

She used the upended bucket to reach the window ledge. From there, she tested the bars.

One was slightly loose.

She could work with that, and began scraping the spot where it fit into the concrete wall. Twenty minutes later, she acknowledged that she wasn't getting anywhere. The concrete wall was too dense. And, even if she managed to get one bar out of the way, the space was still too narrow for her to fit through.

Think.

Her gaze passed over the cot. Nothing there. Then she reconsidered. Did it have springs? She turned it over and found that it did. Though her fingers were already scraped raw from digging into the concrete, she struggled to pry a spring from the cot.

By the time she finished, her fingers and hands were bleeding freely. With an impatient swipe, she rubbed them against her pant legs. After a great deal of pushing and bending, she fashioned the spring into a credible weapon. It was primitive, even crude, but it could do damage if she had to defend herself.

It could slice into a man's arm or even take out an eye if wielded properly. It didn't exactly level the playing field—not when her captors had automatic weapons—but it at least gave her something with which to fight back. If her captors thought she would meekly submit to their plans for her, they were in for a surprise.

She stuck the makeshift weapon into her pocket and waited.

When Jameson returned, she was tempted to use the weapon on him, but she decided to bide her time.

"C'mon," he said.

"Where are you taking me?"

"To see your boyfriend. Maybe he can convince you to tell me what I want to know."

She fingered the metal spring. And prepared to do battle when the time came.

* * *

Slowly, painfully, Gideon came to and found himself in a cell with Brianna. Setting his jaw, he fought through the worst of the pain.

"How are you?" she asked. She'd torn a sleeve from her shirt and was using it to dab at his wounds. "Sorry. Dumb question."

"I'll live." It was supposed to be a joke, but judging from her expression, it didn't come off as funny.

"Why did they put us together?" she asked.

While Gideon was grateful to see that Brianna was all right, he also wondered why they had been brought to the same cell. The usual protocol in hostage situations was to keep prisoners apart.

Before he could respond, one of the men stopped his pacing in front of the cell. "What do you think of your new home?" He cackled at his own joke.

Angry burns covered the man's face, and Gideon recalled Briana throwing a pot of boiling water in the face of one of her attackers.

"Nasty-looking burns," Gideon taunted through clenched teeth.

The man glared at Brianna. "I'm looking forward to paying your girlfriend back for them."

She didn't reply, and Gideon held his peace. Silently he vowed that the man would never get his hands on her. Anything he said was likely to get him cuffed at the back of the head again. Better that he save his energy for finding a way out of here.

But he couldn't resist asking one question. "Is Jameson calling the shots?"

"Wouldn't you like to know?"

The guard walked away, still laughing.

"What are we going to do?" she asked when they were alone.

"I don't know. Yet. But we'll find a way out." He wished he felt as confident as he sounded.

The SEAL motto—*adapt and overcome*—came to mind. He looked around the narrow cell, so small that he had to stoop if he wanted to stand. How was he supposed to adapt? Or overcome?

He pushed the negative thoughts from his mind. SEALs didn't try. They succeeded. The maxim had been drummed into his mind by a hardheaded instructor who had given his men no choice but to get the job done.

Don't like where you're at, the square-jawed teacher would challenge his group of tadpoles at Coronado, California. *Change it.* And to Gideon personally: *Stratham, get your rear in gear and get it done.*

The instructor's voice pounded through Gideon's head. *Get it done.*

He started thinking with his training rather

than his fear. The fear wasn't for himself. Never for himself. But for Brianna. What would happen to her if Jameson and his goons killed him first? The images were too horrific to contemplate.

He'd spent months in SERE training, where techniques had been drilled into him to prevent him from being captured and what to do if he was. Survival. Evasion. Resistance. Escape.

Patience was key if you were being held for political reasons and would probably be traded at some point in the future. In that case, you held on and waited it out, no matter how much you wanted to charge full speed ahead.

But if your captors would likely kill you once you'd served your purpose, you took any opportunity to escape, even if it meant risking everything. After all, if your life was unimportant after a certain length of time, you had nothing to lose if you attempted escape.

Gideon had no doubt that he was totally dispensable once Jameson had gotten what he wanted. In fact, a live operative was a distinct liability. Jameson was many things, but one thing he was not was a fool.

Gideon swiped his hand across his temple where one of Jameson's men had pistol-whipped him and wasn't surprised that it came away bloody. He'd had worse and likely would again before this was over.

He had no doubt that Jameson and his men intended to kill him and Brianna. The question was not *if* but *when*. The answer came quickly: when they ceased to be of value.

SEVENTEEN

Jameson was unraveling.

It was there in his constant pacing, in the way he smacked his gum, in the twitching of his hands, as though no part of his body was allowed to remain still. When his hands stopped twitching, he wrapped his arms around himself while still managing to maintain a grip on his weapon.

Gideon harnessed all the control at his command. Having Brianna anywhere near Rex Jameson made his blood curdle.

He'd swaggered into the hallway outside the cells a few minutes ago. The way the other men moved out of his way spoke volumes about the fear he used to control them. No one wanted to be on his bad side.

Jameson entered the cell and Gideon watched the man's hold on his gun, and himself, grow more tenuous. Jameson was unpredictable at best. He could easily pull the trigger for no other reason than temper.

Jameson kicked him in the ribs. "The boss said I could play with you."

The boss? Wasn't Jameson the boss?

Gideon didn't have time to puzzle over that comment as the man kicked him again. His ribs ached abominably; he wouldn't be surprised if a couple of them were broken.

"You caused me no end of trouble. You thought you were so smart, finding me and then sending me to Alcatraz of the Rockies. Do you know what it's like in there? Twenty-three out of twenty-four hours a day locked in a cell no bigger than a closet. No daylight. No one to shoot the breeze with. Nothing but walls. And cold like I'd never known."

"You did that to yourself," Brianna said.

Though Gideon appreciated the support, he wished she hadn't said anything. No way did he want Jameson to turn his temper on her.

The man took a step in her direction, arm raised.

Gideon held his breath. At the same time he saw Brianna strike out with something curled in her hand to slice at Jameson's cheek.

He yowled. "What did you do to me?" He pulled her hand open and exposed a bedspring. "I ought to use this on you, slice open that pretty face of yours."

Gideon feared he was going to do just that, but

at the last moment, Jameson altered his direction, came at him and kicked him in the ribs again.

"You deserve everything that's coming to you. You and your pretty girlfriend."

Gideon rolled to the other side, agony screaming through his body. But he wasn't out. Not yet. His fingers scrabbled over the rough floor, searching for something—anything—to use as a weapon.

He found it in a broken chunk of cement and closed his fingers over it.

This time when Jameson aimed another kick at him, he summoned his last ounce of strength and threw the piece of cement at his attacker. It hit Jameson in the temple. Blood trickled from the wound, and he paused to swipe at it with the back of his hand. Rage flared in his eyes, promising retribution.

Gideon didn't deceive himself. He was in bad shape. If Jameson got in another kick, he wouldn't be able to defend himself.

But giving up wasn't in his vocabulary. He inhaled deeply and, on the exhale, stumbled to his feet and lunged at the stunned Jameson. At the same time, Brianna took on a guard who had rushed into the cell.

Momentum took him and Jameson down to the ground, where they wrestled over the gun. With his energy nearly depleted, Gideon knew he didn't stand much likelihood of winning, but he wouldn't give up.

Jameson gained control of the gun and pointed it at Gideon's chest.

When the shot went off, he wasn't certain at first whether he had taken the bullet. With all the injuries he'd already sustained, it was difficult to tell. It took several seconds to realize that the bullet had found Jameson.

He looked up and saw their rescuer in the doorway. "Am I glad to see you."

Berrot Newhouse smiled down at him.

Brianna stared at the marshal she'd once dated. They'd gone out only a few times, and though she'd sensed he'd wanted more, something had held her back. Unaccountably a drip of fear slid through her, and her inner antennae started to quiver. "Th—" She wet her dry lips and tried again. "Thank you for finding us."

Newhouse's lips turned up in a self-satisfied smile, his expression alarming her. "It wasn't that hard," he said. "Especially since I'm the one who arranged your kidnapping."

Had she heard correctly? "You?"

"Sure."

Now the smug expression made sense.

Newhouse divided a look between Gideon and her. "Couldn't let him kill you."

"You're the traitor?" she asked.

A slight incline of his head answered her question.

She directed a derisive look his way. "I should have known. You were always weak." She understood him well enough to know that being labeled weak was something he couldn't live with.

"Be careful. You wouldn't like what I can do when a *friend* insults me."

"Friend?" She tossed the word back at him with a sneer.

Gideon hadn't said anything until now, and she knew that he was trying to accept the idea that a fellow marshal had betrayed them. "Why not let Jameson kill us?" he asked now.

"I still need you." Newhouse looked anything but happy at the admission. "You and Brianna both have things to tell us. First, you're going to tell us what Nate told you."

"We've been through this."

"I didn't believe you then and I don't believe you now." Newhouse pulled back his fist and slammed it into Gideon's gut.

Gideon grunted but didn't respond.

"Why kill Jameson?" she asked.

"He'd outlived his usefulness." Newhouse shrugged. "Not my call. Came from higher up."

Brianna had put it together. "You got him out

of jail to do your dirty work and then you killed him."

"Got it in one."

She sent a look of pure revulsion at him. "I knew there was something wrong about you."

"Too bad you didn't stick with me. I'm going places. You could have lived the good life."

She glared at him with contempt. "How did you ever call yourself a marshal?"

"I still am a marshal. A good one. But I got tired of watching scum like Jameson pull in hundreds of thousands of dollars while I was barely scraping by."

"Is that supposed to be an excuse for betraying your friends and everything you once believed in?"

"Take it for what you will. Besides," he added with an unmistakable *gotcha*, "you got nothing to feel so almighty righteous about. Not with your man in on it with us."

What was he talking about?

"Jack?"

"Yeah. Jack. He was as dirty as they came. You had to know about it, you being his wife and all. So don't go getting all high-and-mighty with me."

"Don't listen to him, Brianna."

Newhouse aimed a fist at Gideon's face and

connected with a jaw-shattering blow. "If you know what's good for you, you'll shut up."

She had no intention of listening to a traitor like Newhouse. "You're lying." Jack hadn't been a good husband, at least not at the end, but he'd always been an outstanding marshal. She wouldn't let this man degrade him that way.

"If I'm lying, how do you account for the last five botched operations that he was on?"

"Operations go sideways all the time." But she recalled her own doubts about an op that Jack had been involved in shortly before he'd been killed. It had been straightforward, should have gone off without a hitch, but something had happened and a marshal had been injured. Could Jack have had a hand in that?

No.

It wasn't possible. But she couldn't stop the niggling voice that reminded her of other things that hadn't made sense, like Jack's sudden insistence that she never answer his phone. He'd gone so far as to put password protection on it.

She had to know the truth. For Jack's sake. For her own.

"When did Jack join your merry band of thieves?"

"Three years before he died."

Three years. That had been around the time he had started becoming so critical of her and surly about her promotions. Could the two be connected? Had a guilty conscience prompted Jack's pettiness and jealousy whenever she'd been singled out for recognition and he'd been passed over?

"Jack really came through for us," Berrot continued, "especially when he was in charge of an op. He made sure those ops went bad. That's how he made his money. And it was a good chunk of change. It's funny that he never spent any of it. I always figured he had it holed up somewhere so when he dumped you, you couldn't get your hands on it."

Jack couldn't have had any extra money. They'd had to scrape together every dime they could to make the down payment on the house they'd bought three years before his death. Each month thereafter they were barely getting by after making the mortgage payment. Would he have been so greedy as to hold back money when they so desperately needed it?

Her meandering thoughts startled her. She was obviously more shaken than she'd believed. She'd never have used the money if she'd known it was dirty. That drew her up short. Was she even considering that Jack had been crooked?

Their marriage deserved better than that. They'd made vows to each other, and though the marriage hadn't lasted, she'd meant those vows with all her heart.

Head high, she stared down Newhouse. "What money? We never had anything more than our salaries."

"You don't need to keep up the pretense. Jack took in over seven hundred and fifty grand just for three operations I know of. And that doesn't count what he stole from the organization."

"You're lying," she said again. "If that was true, someone would have noticed. The money would have been discovered."

"Not if he hid it away." Her captor's eyes narrowed in speculation. "Or maybe you did it. Nobody was going to look at the poor little widow, not when everyone felt so sorry for her. I remember you in court, all in black, so brave, so fragile. Who was going to suspect you?"

The derision in his tone caused her to recoil. What had she ever done to him to cause him to hate her so much?

"You think I took the money? You don't know me at all. You never did."

"You and me could have had something good between us," Berrot said, and, for an instant, only the barest of instants, she thought she saw real regret in his eyes. "But you were too good for the likes of me. If you'd ever looked at me, really looked, things might have been different. *I* might have been different."

Was *that* why he despised her? Because she'd

chosen Jack over him? "You're blaming me because you chose to betray everything you said you believed in? I don't think so. You don't get off that easy."

Any sorrow she might have felt for him quickly vanished.

"You think you're too good to have dipped into Jack's stash? Nobody's that good. You'd have taken it same as the rest of us."

"There was never any money." She had a hysterical desire to laugh.

"Jack stashed it somewhere. Maybe he had a girlfriend on the side."

"Jack wasn't like that." But what of the evenings, and there were many, when he was gone? He'd claimed he was catching up on paperwork, but that had never rung true. Jack would palm off filling out reports on anyone he could con into doing it. It had been an office joke that he was allergic to paperwork.

Berrot's eyes turned knowing. "I see you're catching on."

"I don't believe you."

He grinned, but there was a meanness behind it, meanness and triumph. "You don't have to." He jerked up his thumb. "Come on. The boss wants to see you."

"The boss? But Jameson—"

"You thought Jameson was the boss. You really don't have a clue, do you?" His smirk widened, and he pointed to Gideon. "Maybe you'll talk to save him."

Her heart ratcheted up its beat. What would happen to Gideon when Newhouse realized she had no idea where the money was?

Gideon tried to wrap his mind around the idea that a man he'd worked with, even liked, was a traitor. How could Newhouse be part of the criminal enterprise that had operated throughout the West for more than a decade?

Gideon stared at his one-time friend. Though he and Berrot had never been close the way he and Nate had been, they had been colleagues and had respected each other. Or so he'd thought. Now he wondered how he could have been so easily fooled.

Had he seen only what he wanted to see, been duped by the man's easy manner?

"Why? Why join Jameson and his gang?" he asked before Berrot could take Brianna away.

"Oldest reason in the world. Money. Do you think I wanted to live on a civil servant's salary for the rest of my life with peanuts for a pension? I gave my all to the marshals for twelve years and what did I get in return? Shot at. Nearly killed more times than I can count. I deserved something for risking my life over and over."

"You came from money. You didn't need more."

Newhouse laughed as though that was the funniest thing he'd ever heard. "I never figured you for a fool, Stratham. Looks like I was wrong. The 'family money' ran out years ago. I have expensive tastes and I like to indulge them."

"How did it happen?"

"Ten years ago, one of the big players from California came to me and made me a proposition I couldn't refuse. All I had to do was to feed him and his partners some information once in a while. No big deal."

"Information like the location of certain key witnesses?"

Newhouse gave a what-do-you-think? shrug. "It wasn't much at first. Gradually, it grew as I proved what I could do. I was so good at my job that I was promoted. Now I'm the 2IC for the whole southwest operation. Everything that happens goes through me before I kick it on upstairs to the boss."

"You're bragging about it?" Gideon couldn't keep the incredulity out of his voice. Being second-in-command was nothing if it meant throwing away every value you'd ever had.

Another shrug on Newhouse's part. "Why shouldn't I? I rose fast in the organization and the big boys rewarded me." His mouth compressed into a hard line. "Not like with the marshals, where the powers that be parse out promotions like they're made of gold."

"So where did Jameson fit in?"

"The boys on the West Coast wanted Jameson taught a lesson. He thought he was running things on his own and refused to take orders. I orchestrated his capture. Who do you think gave the tip to his location that night you brought him in?"

"Why?" Gideon felt like he was still a step behind.

"Because I knew what would happen when he was put on trial. The fool would make his stupid threats. All I had to do was whisper in his ear what he was already feeling. He did the rest."

Gideon did his best to fit the pieces together. "Jameson was never calling the shots, was he?"

"No. He was strictly an errand boy. He made noises like he was the boss and had a way with him that made others listen. It didn't hurt that he was bigger than everyone else, but when it came right down to it, he was an enforcer. Nothing more."

"Am I going to meet the number-one man?" Gideon asked.

"Anytime now."

"Something's been bothering me. How did you get that note on my truck? You didn't have a tracker on us by then."

"Easy. We let it get around that we were looking for you. With enough money to spread around, it wasn't hard to get enough eyes on the street to find you. I told them what I wanted the note to read." Newhouse's gaze turned hard. "You didn't obey instructions, though, and brought Brianna with you. She was supposed to stay behind so that we could grab her."

Gideon turned it over in his mind. "So I was supposed to die and leave Brianna to you."

"Yeah. It would have solved two problems. Taking you out and leaving her vulnerable so that we could force her to tell us where the money was. Instead, you lived through it and we couldn't get our hands on her."

Gideon shot his one-time friend a look of disgust. "You're worse than the scum I used to put away."

Newhouse reared back and slugged Gideon in the jaw.

He ran his tongue over his teeth and discovered a couple were loose. "What about Nate? Was that you?"

"Yeah. I guess I should feel bad about that, but guess what?" He grinned widely. "I don't. Saxton was always such a Boy Scout when it came to doing what was right. I approached him once, just making small talk about the money he'd make if he jumped sides. He looked at me kind of strange. I laughed it off, told him I was only kidding, but things were different between us after that."

Gideon could only imagine Nate's bafflement at Berrot's offer. "You killed him because of that?"

"That and his determination to bring in Jameson. We needed Jameson free so that he could take out the people who stood in our way.

"The judge had started looking in to the whole chain-of-evidence thing. I couldn't have that. Eventually, he'd discover that I'd planted the false chain of evidence."

"And what about the others Jameson killed?"

"Collateral damage. I didn't want to draw attention to Judge Racine. Someone else needed to die, too."

"And Brianna?"

A nasty smile settled in Newhouse's eyes. "That was for me."

What did he mean by that?

"For you?"

"She and I went out a few times back before she met Jack. She dumped me and started seeing Jack. That was the end of it. She'd have been a lot better off with me."

"And for that you ordered Jameson to kill her."

"It didn't take much convincing. Of course, we can't kill her until we get the location of the money from her."

"I never saw it before," Gideon said thoughtfully, "but you're a coward. Even more of one than Jameson."

Newhouse's eyes narrowed, and his mouth turned mean. "You've either got a lot of nerve or a lot of dumb things to say that, given the circumstances."

"I figure you're gonna kill me either way. Might as well get it off my chest."

"There's dying and then there's dying."

Gideon got it. Fast and easy, or slow and hard. He had no doubt which Newhouse would choose.

EIGHTEEN

Toria Callahan sauntered in at that moment. "Surprised?" The question was directed to Gideon and Brianna.

Brianna raised her chin. "Not really."

"You're making that up. You couldn't have known." Anger glared from her carefully made up eyes.

"Am I?"

A vein in Callahan's forehead pulsed. She inhaled deeply, seeming to breathe herself under control, then set her gaze on Gideon. "What about you?"

"Once I knew that Berrot was in on it, it made sense that you were, too. He couldn't have operated under your nose without you knowing about it. You're too smart for that."

She preened a bit. "You're right. I am too smart for that."

"Too bad you're not smart enough to know that you're going to the same place he is."

The tightening of the lines fanning from the corners of her eyes told Brianna that the woman didn't like that. "I find I don't care for your sense of humor."

Gideon laughed. "And here I thought I was being really funny."

"Were you dirty at the DEA as well?" Brianna asked.

Callahan gave a slight dip of her head. "I was approached by one of the big boys in a crime syndicate. When I made the move to the marshals, I continued with my little side job." She gestured toward Newhouse. With a malevolent look at Gideon, he took off.

"I'm glad you sent him out," Brianna said. "In the end, he's only hired help, isn't he?"

"You're quick. Too bad you and I never worked together. I think we'd have gotten along just fine."

Brianna curled her lip. "I don't think so. I have a thing about snakes."

Callahan drew back her arm and slapped her.

Brianna wiped blood from her mouth. "You and Newhouse have obviously been working both sides of the street for a long time. I hope you got what you wanted."

"There's never enough for someone motivated by greed," Gideon said.

Callahan tossed back her head. "I have a right to have some of the good things in life, things like the people we routinely put away take for granted. There's nothing wrong with that."

"Who are you trying to convince?" Brianna asked. "Us? Or yourself?"

Rage flared in the woman's eyes.

Gideon had been right. Greed was behind everything the woman had done.

"You threw away everything you once believed in."

"I did what I had to. Don't tell me you wouldn't have done the same thing."

"I didn't sell my badge for a pile of money. And I didn't betray my friends." Brianna skewed her with a look of pure loathing. "You set Nate up to be killed. How do you live with yourself?"

"Very well." Callahan skimmed her fingers down her obviously expensive blouse. "Exceptionally well, in fact."

Brianna thought of the woman's cashmere coat. "Cashmere doesn't come cheap, does it?"

"No. It doesn't. You think you and Stratham can stop me? Think again. When I get the money Jack stole from us, I'll be leaving the country to somewhere without an extradition treaty." Triumph and greed turned her face into that of a cartoon character. "All you have to do is tell me where you and Jack stashed the money. Simple."

"How many times do I have to tell you that I don't have the money?"

"Why didn't you come after Brianna until now?" Gideon asked.

"We thought Jameson stole the money and decided to let him sit in a cell until we needed it. There was nothing he could do with it, and neither Newhouse nor I could be seen with a big pile of money. The Feds tend to frown on that." Her laugh was caustic. "I could wait for my 'retirement fund.'"

"What changed?"

"There was a rumor going around that Jameson was going to meet with the authorities. We couldn't have that. We had to get him out so that we could get the money before he gave it up. Also, he made a convenient scapegoat for taking out Racine.

"The trouble was that Jameson convinced us he never had the money and that it had to have been Jack who took it." Callahan sent a nasty smile Brianna's way. "You'll tell us where the money is. One way or the other."

How could she tell Callahan and Newhouse where the money was when she had no idea?

"Maybe this will help jog your memory." Callahan held her weapon to Gideon's temple. "I've seen how you look at Stratham. You have feelings for him. Anyone can see it. Jack saw it, even joked about it to me. He said it made sense—two Goody Two-shoes like you being attracted to each other. Could be that's why he decided to throw in with us."

Brianna bit her tongue hard enough to draw blood, trying to hold herself together. Even so, panic clawed at her throat as her gaze was riveted on the barrel of the gun pressed against Gideon's temple. "That's not true.

"What Jack did, he did for himself. He never knew—" She stopped abruptly. Never by word or deed had she let on to Jack that she had feelings for his partner. She'd never even admitted it to herself. Could Jack have seen what she'd refused to acknowledge?

"Never knew what? That you were in love with his partner?"

"I wasn't." But her words lacked conviction.

"Then you won't mind if I pull the trigger."

"Please. Don't do this." She swallowed. "I don't have your money. I never had it. I'd give it to you if I did."

"Not so arrogant now, are you?" Callahan taunted. She lowered her arm and turned to Newhouse. "I think she's telling the truth. There's no way she could hold out against Stratham being killed. If Jack took the money, he didn't tell his little wife. She's clueless about it."

"So why are we keeping them alive?" Newhouse demanded.

Callahan didn't answer.

What was going to happen now that Callahan had decided she didn't have the money? Brianna refused to let her thoughts go there. Instead, they lingered on Callahan's accusation that she was in love with Gideon.

What must he be thinking? Could they have a life together? With Ruthie and then other children to come?

The picture her mind painted was so vivid that she could see the home they'd make, one filled with love and laughter, a home very different from that which she'd shared with Jack.

She wanted that. Callahan and Newhouse weren't going to take it from her.

"You're a fool, Stratham," Newhouse said as he marched them toward the cells. "All that courage, honor and integrity stuff you picked up from your SEAL days didn't save you, did they? If you had any sense, you'd know that money talks louder than any of those stale words. Instead, you're still working for peanuts at some mom-and-pop security firm."

Gideon ignored the slur against S&J. He had more important things to deal with—like how to get him and Brianna out of here. "At least I can look at myself in the mirror."

"I like what I see just fine when I look at myself."

"We'll see how you like yourself in prison orange."

Newhouse turned to the guard with the burned face. "Make them comfortable, Bob."

While another guard stood watch, Bob tossed them inside the cell, but not before tying their hands behind their backs and covering their mouths with duct tape. Bob had taken extra pleasure in binding their hands as tightly as possible.

Gideon didn't mind for himself, but he winced with every jerk of the rope around Brianna's wrists.

In his mind he had weighed various plans for escape and had come up with one that seemed to have the lowest possibility of getting him and Brianna killed. Right now, he'd take that as a good thing.

The first order of business was to get the tape off his mouth. His plan wouldn't work if he couldn't talk. He rubbed his mouth back and forth against the rough stone wall, scraping the tape. He felt an edge give way and continued to scrape his lips along a ridge of stone. It was painstaking work, and he figured he was scrubbing off a couple of layers of skin along with the tape.

When he managed to get the tape free, he spat it to the ground, not surprised to see flecks of blood and whiskers sticking to the back side.

He moved his mouth back and forth to get it working again. When he had enough saliva that he could talk, he whispered to Brianna, "Don't react. I've got a plan." Then he called to the guard.

"Hey, Bob. Come over here. I've got a proposition for you."

The bored-looking guard didn't move, only raised an eyebrow. "You got the tape off, did you? Too bad it won't do you any good."

"It might do you some good."

The guard picked his teeth with a toothpick. "You ain't got nothin' I want."

"You won't know until you hear what I have to say."

Another eyebrow lift. "And what would that be?"

"I'm thinking you're all hat and no cattle," Gideon said. "You've been itching to get your hands on me, haven't you? Why not now?"

"You ain't as smart as you think you are, 'cause you ain't getting me to open that cell for you."

"No problem." Gideon shrugged. "I figured you for a coward. Afraid to take on a man. Women are more your style, aren't they?"

The man's nostrils flared. "You saying that I'm a coward?"

Gideon bobbled his head. "That's exactly what I'm saying."

"Nobody's ever said that before and lived."

"Well, I'm saying it now."

"Mister, you're a fool," the second guard said. "Bob, here, will take you apart limb by limb. He don't cotton to folks calling him a coward."

Gideon didn't doubt it, but he had to get his hands on one of the bullets.

"You want to say that when you're not tucked all safe and sound inside a cell?" Bob asked.

"Happy to."

"Bob, don't do it," the other man said. "He's just baiting you. Anything happens to him and the boss'll have your hide."

"Don't care. Nobody talks to me like that and gets away with it."

"Is that so, B-o-o-ob?" Gideon drew out the man's name in a deliberate taunt.

"That's it. You're going to get what you have coming to you."

"Yeah? Prove it." Gideon lifted an eyebrow when Bob remained where he was. "That's what I thought. You're yellow all the way through."

Bob undid the lock to the cell and yanked Gideon out. "Are you ready to put your fists where you mouth is?"

Gideon knew he was in for a beating. That was okay. As long as he got what he wanted, he'd take his lumps.

"You gonna undo my hands?" he asked. "Or are you gonna pound on me when I can't fight back?" He raked Bob with a contemptuous look. "That's your style, isn't it?"

Bob gestured to the other guard. "Undo his hands."

The man backed up. "I ain't havin' nothin' to do with this. You want to undo his hands, you do it. If the boss finds out about this, she'll not only have your hide, she'll pin it to the wall. I'm not giving her reason to pin mine there, too."

Muttering under his breath, Bob undid Gideon's hands. "Let's do this."

Bob started pounding on him. With fists the size of shovels, he made a formidable opponent.

Gideon did his best to block the man's punches or dance out of their way, but he couldn't avoid them altogether, especially if he wanted to get the prize: a bullet from the cross-holster Bob wore across his chest. It was a macho thing, but some men thought it enhanced their tough-guy image. Clearly Bob was one of those men.

Gideon moved in close, got in a few jabs to the man's midsection and managed to surreptitiously grab a bullet from his bandolier. He'd have liked to end it there, but Bob wanted his pound of flesh. Gideon had challenged him in front of the other man. That kind of slight didn't go unpunished.

He'd gone over it in his mind. Though he didn't doubt he could take Bob and the second guard, he didn't know how many others were close. They were likely clustered somewhere nearby and would come running at the first sign of commotion.

His best opportunity for survival was to take the beating and let his opponent have the victory. He feigned being knocked out and fell to the ground.

Bob kicked him over and over.

It took everything he had not to fight back. He just curled in a fetal position, taking every blow and kick with seeming meekness.

"C'mon, Bob," the second guard said. "You're gonna kill him for sure. The boss has plans for him."

Bob kicked Gideon in the head for good measure. "Remember who gave you that beating," he said, "when you're able to think again." He hauled Gideon up by the shoulders and tossed him back inside the cell.

Fortunately Bob was so overcome with the glow of victory that he'd forgotten to bind Gideon's hands and tape up his mouth again, just as he'd hoped.

Gideon fell to the floor and just lay there, needing time to recover before he put the next part of his plan into action. Every inch of his body hurt, and he had to remind himself to breathe past the pain.

Breathe in.

Breathe out.

The rhythm steadied him, and he felt able to get to a sitting position, not an easy feat when every inch of him ached. Pain speared through him with each tiny movement, but he had no choice but to ignore it.

Awkwardly, Brianna knelt beside him. She'd managed to pull the tape from her mouth. "Gideon. Can you hear me?"

The anguish in her voice nearly did him in. "I'm okay. Give me a couple of minutes, and then I'll tell you what we're going to do."

After a few more minutes of steady breathing, he turned his back to the cell door and began taking apart the bullet, meticulously funneling the gunpowder into a small square of cloth he'd torn from his shirt. The precious gunpowder made a neat little package.

He didn't need to explain to Brianna what he was doing. The understanding in her eyes told him she got it.

The next part of his plan would be the hardest to execute. He had to wait and do nothing until night came when guards usually went on a skeleton shift. Those assigned for the midnight shift were likely to be drowsy, maybe even careless, both essential for Gideon's plan to work.

"Get some sleep," he said gently. "You're going to need it."

"Gideon…"

The poignancy in her voice held the knowledge that they might not survive the coming showdown.

He had no answer, and her nod told him she understood.

Several hours later, he roused himself and told Brianna, "Pull the cot over you." He stuffed the cloth into the cell lock, used a broken piece of concrete to pound it in more tightly.

In no time the gunpowder blew the lock.

"You all right?" he asked as he wiped dust and soot from his face.

"Fine." She coughed. "Let's get out of here."

Gideon took out the first guard with no problem. When the next appeared, Brianna gave him a hard chop to the back of his neck.

Footsteps sounded in the passageway leading to the cells. More guards, he figured. But it wasn't more guards who appeared. It was Callahan and Newhouse.

"Did you really think you'd get away with your little jailbreak?" Callahan taunted. "When I heard about your fight with Bob, I knew there was something going on. It didn't take much to figure out that you were planning to escape. So I waited."

Newhouse smirked and pointed his weapon at Brianna. "She convinced us that she doesn't have the money. So there's no reason to keep you two alive."

Gideon pushed her behind him. "Let her go. She has a little girl."

Callahan erupted in laughter. "She's useless to me. Just like you." Without warning, Callahan turned her weapon on her partner. "And you." She pulled the trigger.

Gideon stared at the cold-eyed woman with whom he'd once worked.

"I'll find the money eventually. And when I do, I won't have to share it with anyone. Newhouse was a whiner. Always worrying about what we're going to do next. I only kept him around because he was useful, like in getting rid of Jameson. But, like you two, he'd outlived his usefulness."

Callahan aimed her weapon at Gideon, point-blank. There was no way to escape, and he braced himself.

At the last moment, Brianna pushed him aside. The bullet had found a different target.

"No!" The single syllable tore from his throat. He ripped the gun from Callahan's hand, causing it to go off in the struggle, and managed to get in a blow that knocked her out.

He tucked the gun at the back of his waist and ran to Brianna. What he saw caused his heart to clench. Blood gushed from the wound to her side.

He tore a sleeve from his shirt and pressed it to the wound. When the blood kept coming, he tore off the other sleeve and replaced the blood-soaked cloth with it.

When Callahan stirred, he fixed a hard gaze at her and lowered his voice to a menacing pitch. "Make another move, and it'll be your last."

NINETEEN

Brianna tried to make sense of things, but her thoughts were too jumbled.

She'd been shot. At least, she thought she had. The pain was so enormous that she wasn't certain because her brain wasn't working.

Her mind rejected the idea. It wasn't possible that she'd taken a bullet, was it? She had to get back to Ruthie. And Miso. She'd made a promise, and she always kept her promises.

She remembered a burst of gunfire shattering the air. Then the noise had stopped, and the pain had begun. She'd read what it felt like to be shot, but reading about it and experiencing it were two different things.

Something startled her out of her thoughts. What had she been thinking about, anyway? She must have blacked out for a minute. Or more. Time had no meaning in her disoriented state.

The world was spinning. No, that wasn't right. It was falling, and she was falling with it into a sea of darkness and intense cold. She shivered uncontrollably.

She was so cold that it was hard to think. She pulled back her thoughts and let them drift. There. That was better. She needed to rest. Once she did, the world would set itself right again, and she'd find that she hadn't been shot at all.

Satisfied, she allowed her mind to move on to happier things. Like seeing Ruthie again.

"Open your eyes." Gideon's voice. At least, she thought it was his voice. She did her best to block everything else and focused on the sound of his voice.

If she could hold on to that, she knew she'd be all right.

"Brianna, you're going to be all right. You're not going anywhere, and neither am I."

There was Gideon's voice again. She tried to focus, but her concentration was shot. Oh, that was funny. She'd been shot, and her concentration was shot.

She wanted to laugh at the absurdity of it, but she couldn't make her mouth work.

Groaning with the effort, she tried to open her eyes, but they seemed glued shut. Why wouldn't they work? She tried to answer Gideon's plea, but her tongue was thick and wouldn't work any better than her eyes did.

"I'm begging You, Lord, don't let her die." The

words were muffled now, but somehow reached her brain. "Ruthie needs her. I need her. Bless her with Your healing."

Had Gideon just called upon the Lord? But that didn't make sense. Gideon wasn't a believer. How was it that he was praying? She wanted to commend him, to tell him that she was happy that he was praying, but there was still a problem with her tongue. She tried to move it, but it refused.

Why wouldn't it work?

Oh. That's right. She remembered now. She'd been shot. The explanation in place, she felt better and accepted her descent into inky blackness.

Gideon couldn't stop the blood gushing from the wound in Brianna's side no matter how hard he pressed the bloody cloth against it.

"Brianna. Come back to me. Please, come back." His gut clenching with worry, he grabbed Callahan's phone, noted it contained a GPS app, then punched in 911 and barked out the information.

He spared a moment to tie Callahan's hands behind her back. The cowed look in her eyes told him she wasn't going to give him any trouble.

Silently he prayed to the God he thought he no longer believed in, begging for His mercy once again. Heart pounding like a brutal fist inside his chest, he continued to apply pressure and was gratified when the blood flow slowed. He had a feeling if the bullet had been an inch higher, she'd have been dead by now.

Sirens screeched through the night. Paramedics and police arrived at the same time.

"Move aside, sir," a voice ordered.

Gideon couldn't bring himself to move.

"It's all right," the same voice said. "We've got her. We'll take good care of her."

Within seconds, Brianna was strapped to a gurney.

"I'm going with her."

The EMT looked at Gideon, obviously taking his measure, and nodded. "I'm not going to stop you, sir. I have a feeling that's a fight I wouldn't win."

"You're right about that."

He spent a moment filling in the police on what had happened. "You'll need to make a statement," an officer said.

"Later." Gideon climbed in the ambulance. The ride to the hospital was a roller coaster of emotions. He did his best to keep out of the way and let the EMTs work on the woman who held his heart, all the while recalling Callahan's remark about Brianna loving him and her reaction to it. Had Callahan been right or had she only been taunting him?

He thought of the vow he'd made to Ruthie

to keep her mother safe. If Brianna died… The most important promise he'd ever made, and he might break it because of a bullet meant for him.

"Sir," a nurse said, breaking into his thoughts when he entered the ER, "we need to see to you. You look like you've been through a wood-chipper."

Gideon had all but forgotten about his own injuries.

After his ribs were taped up and stinging antiseptic applied to his bruises and scrapes, he was shown to the waiting room, where the smell of pungent cleansers, stale coffee and crushing fear mixed in a nasty brew. Was there anything more excruciating than waiting for news in a hospital? At the moment, he couldn't think of anything. He sat slumped in a molded plastic chair that allowed for no comfortable position. The whisper of crepe-soled shoes and the occasional murmuring of voices provided a backdrop to his tormented thoughts.

When the doctor appeared four hours later, he bolted upright.

"Your friend will be fine," the doctor, a thirty-something woman, said. "She lost a lot of blood, but it could have been worse. Someone—I hear it was you—staunched the blood and probably saved her life doing so. As long as she takes it easy, she'll make a nice recovery."

Gideon absorbed the words, his heart spilling over with gratitude. "When can I see her?"

"Tomorrow morning at the earliest. I suggest you go home and get some rest."

Ignoring that, he settled in the waiting room, prepared to spend the night. A call to Rafe and Shannon alerted them to Brianna's condition. He asked them to tell Ruthie that her mother had been hurt but that she was going to be all right.

By morning, he had decided on a course of action. Though it ripped the heart from him, he didn't have a choice. He didn't doubt that Brianna had feelings for him, but they would fade when he got out of her life. He loved her too much to subject her to the memories his presence would foster.

First, her husband had died on his watch, and even though Jack had been dirty, Gideon couldn't help regretting the way he'd died. If that wasn't enough, Brianna had been shot and almost died, again on his watch. She'd be better off without him.

It was that simple. And that complicated.

How could he be with a woman like Brianna, who was light and life, while he feared his soul would be forever shrouded in darkness? Though he was working his way back to a relationship with the Lord, he had a long way to go. He was so far from his goal that he felt like he was at the bottom of a well, reaching for the stars and all he could find was a crack in the darkness.

Her belief in the Savior was an integral part of her life. Her absolute faith had never wavered, even when they'd been in the direst of circumstances.

When he was given permission to go in and see her, he did so with a forced smile and more trepidation than he believed possible.

Pale, with her hair swept back from her face, she looked fragile. To his eyes, though, she was more lovely than ever.

"You're beautiful."

The wry smile she sent his way told him what she thought of that. "You need to have your eyesight examined. I look like I've been shot." She reached for the water glass on the side table and winced.

"Let me." He handed the glass to her and wondered how he was going to tell her that he was walking out of her life.

"Thank you," she said. "You saved my life. The doctor told me if you hadn't stopped the bleeding when you did that I wouldn't be here."

"Seems to me it's the other way around. That bullet was meant for me." He swallowed. "Why did you push me to the side?"

She gave him a long study. "Why do you think?"

"You could have died." There. He'd said the words that had stuck in his throat for the last twenty-four hours.

"Did you want me to stand by and let you be shot? Callahan had you directly in her sights. I thought I could get us both out of the way." Her smile was wry. "Turns out that I was wrong."

When he didn't answer, she said, "Hey, I'm going to be all right. If you don't believe me, ask the doctor."

"I did." In fact, he'd asked the doctor so many times that the woman had told him in plain and simple words that Brianna would be fine and to stop pestering her.

"I talked with Shannon and Rafe," he added. "They're bringing Ruthie to see you when you're up to it."

Brianna made a face. "In a couple of days maybe I won't look so bad. I don't want her seeing me when I look like this."

"You know that wouldn't matter to her."

"I know. But it does to me."

He could only guess at how much she wanted to see Ruthie, but, once again, Brianna's first thoughts were of her daughter, trying to protect her as much as possible from the hard fact that her mother had been shot.

"You are the bravest person I've ever known," he said.

"Outside of your SEAL buddies?"

"No. Just what I said." He searched for another subject. "Turns out Callahan didn't kill Newhouse after all. He's going to make a full recovery."

"I hope they spend the rest of their lives behind bars."

"You and me both. Those two don't deserve any deals. Not after what they've done. When I think of the lives they cost..." He stopped. They'd almost cost Brianna her life. Which brought him back to why he was here.

"You'll be able to get back to your life pretty soon," he said, trying for casual. "I guess that means goodbye for us."

"Goodbye?" The word held confusion and something else. Hurt?

"You don't need me anymore. Jameson's dead, and the rest are going to prison."

Her stricken expression nearly tore the heart from him, but he held firm.

He bent to brush a kiss over her cheek. "Goodbye, Brianna." He headed to the door.

"Wait!" she called.

By the way she stretched the word into two syllables, he could tell how confused and hurt she was. He paused, turned and then continued walking, but not before he saw her blinking tears away, her pain flowing into him. He didn't need to wonder why she was crying. After all they'd been through, he was walking out on her. It must seem like a kind of betrayal, just as Jack had betrayed her.

Needing a moment to collect himself, he headed for the men's washroom, splashed cold water on his face and stared at his reflection in the mirror. He didn't see himself; he saw the hurt on Brianna's face.

There were different ways of looking at yourself in the mirror, he decided. One was to open your eyes and see the person you loved staring back at you.

Brianna stared after him. Was he leaving? Just like that? If she'd had the strength, she would have gone after him. Or punched him in the nose.

Didn't he know that she loved him? She'd thought he felt the same.

Had they come through all this only for Gideon to walk out on her? A sob built in her throat. She swallowed it down, but nothing would ease the ache in her heart.

For a few minutes she indulged in an invitation-for-one pity party. Then, with the faith that had gotten her through every crisis in her life, she shored up her resolve. She'd get through this and come out on the other end stronger than ever.

She had Ruthie. What had she told Gideon?

She and Ruthie were a team. They were all each other needed.

She pondered on changing her name back to her original one and decided against it. Leah Fuller no longer existed. She was Brianna Thomas now; she'd earned that name through blood and tears.

Several days later, when Shannon and Rafe brought Ruthie to the hospital, Brianna hugged her daughter so tightly that Ruthie protested.

"Mommy, you're squeezing my heart so it's coming out of my mouth."

Brianna eased up on her hold. "I'm sorry. I'm just so glad to see you."

"You don't look very good," Ruthie said with childlike bluntness.

"I'll look better soon. Promise."

"Okay. Miso wanted to come, too, but Shannon said the hospital probably doesn't allow cats."

"I think Shannon's right." Brianna wanted to ask the couple about Gideon and almost did, but bit back the question before she humiliated herself. Besides, she didn't want to put Rafe and Shannon on the spot.

And that's what it would have been. They'd have had to make excuses as to why Gideon, their friend and boss, hadn't been to see her. The conversation would have been awkward in the extreme.

She caught the sympathy in Shannon's eyes and knew the other woman understood.

When Rafe took Ruthie to the hospital cafeteria for a snack, Shannon filled in Brianna on what was happening with Newhouse and Callahan. "They couldn't turn on each other fast enough and are both trying to cut deals with the DA's office. They'll both stand trial for murder, conspiracy, kidnapping and a host of other charges. I doubt either will be seeing the outside of prison bars. Ever.

"There's other news. When the Feds learned that Jack took the money—" she paused as Brianna winced "—they found it in an account he'd opened up under one of his aliases while he was undercover."

Brianna murmured her satisfaction at that, but it wasn't really what she wanted to talk about. "And Gideon? How is he?"

"Rafe says he's moping around and snaps at anyone who tries to talk to him. Do you want me to tell Rafe to knock him on his keister?"

Brianna forced a smile. "It's tempting. But no."

"I love Gideon. He's like a brother to me, but he's acting like a fool," Shannon said.

Brianna felt bound to defend him. "He protected me and Ruthie. That's what he promised to do. Just because I have feelings for him doesn't mean he has to have them for me."

"You're in love with him." The blunt words stripped off the bandage and exposed the raw wound that was Brianna's heart.

She didn't bother denying it. "We never talked about it, but I thought... I thought he felt the same. Obviously I was wrong."

"I wouldn't be so sure," Shannon said. "He's never taken anyone to his cabin before. Not even Rafe, and they're as close as brothers." She gave Brianna a moment to mull that over.

In fact, it was all she could think about as the long hours in the hospital turned to days with excruciating slowness. Shannon and Rafe brought Ruthie to see Brianna every day. She held on to those visits as she would a lifeline.

"You look better, Mommy," Ruthie said one day. "You don't look so dead anymore."

Rafe and Shannon laughed.

"She's right," Shannon said. "You are looking better."

Brianna managed a smile. "Thanks."

Her body was healing. That was a plus. Her emotions, though, were a jumble of disappointment, hurt and bewilderment. After his initial visit, Gideon hadn't returned. What had she expected? she asked herself with a touch of anger. He'd told her goodbye.

"If you need anything, anything at all from Rafe or me, you have only to ask." Shannon kissed Brianna's cheek. "After all, you and Ruthie are family."

"Family." Brianna held on to the word.

"Can I get into the bed with you?" Ruthie asked.

Brianna flipped back the sheet, and Ruthie climbed in. It was probably against hospital rules, but she didn't care. With her daughter next to her, Brianna knew she'd be all right. She and Gideon had shared a moment...or two...but that was all.

The honest part of her heart called her a liar.

TWENTY

Bam.

    Bam.

    Bam.

Gideon's aim was sure as he put bullet after bullet center mass into the paper target.

The S&J shooting range was a perk of his job, and he took advantage of it whenever he could. Today, he wasn't shooting for practice, but to let out his temper.

He didn't much like himself. Because he didn't, he took it out on his coworkers and everyone else unfortunate enough to be in his vicinity.

Without Brianna, nothing was right. Gideon missed her and Ruthie, and, yes, Miso, too. He missed them with an ache that was more than longing. The void in his life was so deep that he wondered if he could ever move beyond it.

He'd convinced himself that walking away from them was sensible, the only thing he could do, but being sensible hadn't made him happy or quelled the longing he would always feel for them.

The case was over. He had no reason to see them again, no reason to call, no reason for anything.

He'd racked his brain to find something—anything—to give him an excuse to contact Brianna. But came up with nothing. Silence had its own name, he'd discovered, and its name was loneliness.

Never had he felt it so acutely as he did now. The loneliness pressed down on him, a living, breathing thing that caused him to want to cry out, if only to hear the sound of a voice, no matter that it was his own.

He had often felt alone in the world and had accepted it as the way things were, but now, he realized he no longer wanted to accept it. Moreover, he did not have to accept it. He was alone by choice.

You don't ever have to be alone. The Lord is always there if you'll let Him in. The choice is yours.

Brianna's words echoed in his mind.

Gideon's part in bringing the traitors to justice had garnered valuable publicity for S&J Security/Protection, which in turn had earned local, national and even international goodwill for the firm.

Yeah, everything was great, he thought sourly, as he drilled another bullet in the target. But he was still alone. Until, that is, Rafe showed up.

The worry in his friend's eyes alerted Gideon that something was wrong.

"What's happened?"

"Robert Winfield escaped."

It took Gideon a moment to place the name. Robert Winfield. Bob. The man whom Gideon had allowed to beat him to within an inch of his life so that he could get a bullet.

"How?"

"When prisoners were being transferred to Fort Collins, one had a seizure. The guards' attention were all on him, and Winfield just walked out."

"He walked out, and no one stopped him?" Gideon asked incredulously.

"That's the story I got. Someone is going to be walking a beat unless I miss my guess. The locals and the Feds are all over it. Here's the part I don't like. One of the guards had the good sense to question Winfield's cellmate. The man said that all Winfield could talk about was payback for the woman who burned his face."

"Brianna."

Rafe's nod was grim. "Yeah. She's leaving this morning to go back to her home in Silverton. It seems unlikely that Winfield would know where she was headed, but—"

Gideon didn't let him finish. Tendrils of fear coiled in his gut. "I'm going after her." His blood ran hot, but his mind was cold. He couldn't afford to allow anger to blur his thinking.

"Do you want me to tag along?"

"Stay here. See what you can find out about sightings on Winfield and let me know."

Gideon prayed as he ran to his truck. *Please, Lord, let me be in time.*

Brianna didn't plan on rushing the trip to Silverton. She and Ruthie could take their time.

Stowing their few belongings in the car Rafe and Shannon had rented for her, she welcomed the cold of outside, the frigid air stinging her skin. At least it was not sodden with her own tears, as was the recycled air of the hospital room.

It was time to start her life over.

Again.

Once they got on the highway, Ruthie popped a thumb in her mouth and slept, and Brianna let her thoughts wander.

She had come to terms with Jack's betrayal of his badge and pledge to uphold the law as a marshal. Something had been broken inside him, a need to be more, to have more, to take more.

Could she have prevented him from going to the other side if she'd looked more closely, been more aware of those broken parts? She didn't know.

In the end, Jack had made his own choices. And she had made hers.

What of the future?

She didn't doubt that over the coming days and weeks and months she'd struggle to get over the heartbreak that was Gideon.

Tears ran down her face, a river of grief she felt powerless to stem.

Ruthie woke up just as Brianna was wiping tears from her eyes. "Mommy, why are you crying?"

"I don't know."

"I do." Ruthie nodded sagely. "You miss Gideon. I do, too. So does Miso. Why didn't he come with us?"

How did she explain to her daughter that he'd had a life before he'd come back into hers, one that didn't include her and Ruthie?

"I don't know." Was that becoming her default answer?

"I love Gideon. I want him to be part of our family. Could I ask him to be my daddy?"

The tears came harder. "I don't think so."

"Mommy, you don't know a lot of things today."

That earned a small laugh on Brianna's part. "You're right, sweetheart. I don't know a lot of things."

"That's okay. I think you're smart, anyway."

"Thank you."

Unwilling to sink into depression, she counted

her blessings. She had a daughter whom she loved beyond reason, a career as an analyst she could return to and the knowledge that she no longer had to look over her shoulder.

"Where are we going?" Ruthie asked.

"Home."

"Back to our house in Silverton?"

At Brianna's nod, Ruthie frowned. "I liked it at Gideon's place better." She frowned. "Only it burned down."

"That's right."

"It was a good place before the bad men came."

"The bad men can't hurt us anymore," Brianna soothed.

Ruthie nodded sagely. "I know. Because you and Gideon made them go away."

"That's right."

"I miss Gideon. Even if his cat pancakes aren't that good." The plaintive note in her daughter's voice caused a little ache to settle in Brianna's heart.

"So do I," she said softly. "So do I."

"Mommy. Look!" Ruthie pointed to a sign that advertised Colorado's Best Hot Chocolate. "Can we stop?"

"I don't see why not." In truth, Brianna needed a break from driving. Her wound had healed, but she still wasn't at 100 percent.

She found a parking spot, saw to Miso's needs,

then she and Ruthie headed to the country store. After using the restroom, they ordered two hot chocolates.

"It has little marshmallows," Ruthie said. "Like Gideon made." Her excitement died. "I miss Gideon. Even if he didn't say goodbye to me."

Brianna had taken only one sip of her chocolate before pushing it aside. "He had to get back to his other life."

Ruthie stuck out her little chin. "He still should have said goodbye."

"You're right. He should have."

Neither of them finished their hot chocolate.

After making one more stop at the restroom— better safe than sorry—they returned to the car. Just as Brianna was about to open the car door, a figure stepped in front of her.

She recognized him immediately. "Bob."

"That's right. Didn't think you'd see me again, did you?"

Her mind scrambled to make sense of his presence. He was supposed to be in jail. How had he gotten out?

"Ruthie, get behind me and stay there."

"Pretty little girl. Wonder what that pretty face would look like if someone threw boiling water at her."

Brianna didn't think. She threw herself at him. "Ruthie, run! *Run!*"

Bob was ready for her and caught Brianna around the waist.

She twisted free and clawed at his face. Fresh scar tissue was particularly vulnerable, and she didn't hesitate to use her nails to scrape down his cheek.

While he yowled, spraying spittle as he did so, she saw Ruthie taking off to the store.

"You hurt me good the last time we tangled, but you're not getting away," he said and caught her arm, forcing it behind her back. "Not this time."

She recalled her marshal training even as agony tore through her. Use the torque as leverage. She threw her weight to the side, catching him off balance. With that, she kicked backward with her boot-clad foot, hitting him in the knee. She pressed her advantage and slammed her elbow into his gut.

Another yowl on his part.

Unfortunately, she couldn't bring her full strength to bear and hadn't injured him enough to take him down. She spun away and faced him, knees bent, hands up to block any blows.

"You're good," he said, "but you're not good enough." He advanced on her, eyes gleaming with hatred, fists raised.

Her breath came in hard pants, and she knew she wasn't going to get out of this. But she'd make him hurt first.

As long as Ruthie was safe…

Before she finished the thought, strong hands set her aside.

Astonished, she looked up and saw Gideon.

"Let's see how you do with someone your own size." Gideon did his best to keep his rage in check, but seeing Bob about to use his fists on Brianna was enough to shred his self-control.

He picked up the other man and threw him to the ground. Without a wasted movement, he was on top of Bob and began pounding on him.

Feral sounds issued from Bob's throat as he writhed in pain. The blood vessels on his forehead looked ready to pop, while his eyes filled with a hatred so intense that it radiated like a physical thing.

"Gideon. It's all right. I'm all right."

Brianna's voice reached him. She tugged at his arm. "He didn't hurt me."

Gideon stood, pulled flex-cuffs from his pocket and bound Bob's hands. When the man started to whine, Gideon said, "If you know what's good for you, you'll shut up."

He watched Bob's features go slack, until his entire face was drooping heavily.

Hearing footsteps behind him, Gideon turned to see Ruthie, accompanied by an older couple running toward them.

"We've called the police," the woman said, the wailing of a siren punctuating her words.

Ruthie ran to her mother, and Brianna held her close. "Mommy, are you all right?"

"I'm fine." Brianna looked at Gideon. "More than fine."

Ruthie gazed up at Gideon in adoration. "You found us. I knew you would."

"How *did* you find us?" Brianna asked.

"I prayed," he said simply. "And then I saw the sign."

Her gaze softened. "You prayed?"

"I've been praying a lot lately." Whatever else he was going to say was interrupted when Ruthie pulled at his jeans.

"You never said goodbye to me," the little girl said, sadness spilling out from her eyes and running straight into him, lashing his heart with stinging stripes. "I thought we were friends."

"We were. We are," he corrected himself. "I got a little mixed up, but I'm trying to make it right with you."

"O-o-kay," Ruthie said, drawing the word out as though she was considering it. She worried her lower lip with her teeth. "But you better make it right with Mommy first."

Brianna pointed to the car and pressed a button on her key fob. "Why don't you get in the car and play with Miso while Gideon and I talk?"

"But I want to talk with him, too. Gideon wants to make it right with me. Isn't that right?" Ruthie directed the question at him.

"Right. But I really do need to talk with your mom. Then maybe we can talk. Would that be all right?"

"Okay. But don't be too long. I don't know how long I'll feel like talking." Ruthie scampered to the car.

"She's a force of nature," Brianna said with a shake of her head. A wan smile leaked out before it vanished. "How did you know Bob was coming after me?"

"We got word that he escaped as he and other prisoners were being transferred and that he wanted revenge on you. I started after you."

What did he say beyond that? Did he ask her if she'd missed him? Or did he just tell her that he loved her and always would?

There was nothing in S&J's handbook about that.

When she looked at him pointedly, he mustered up all of his courage. "I missed you."

"Did you? Is that why you didn't come to see me? Or call me? Because you missed me?"

The sarcasm stung, but he couldn't object. He deserved that and more. When he didn't say anything, she lifted her chin in challenge.

"I was scared," he said at last. "I didn't know if you'd see me."

"Why wouldn't I?" There was honest bewilderment in her voice.

"I almost got you killed."

"Did you pull the trigger?" At the shake of his head, she said, "Then you didn't almost get me killed. That was Callahan. I needed you when I was in the hospital hurting and scared."

"I let you down. I'm sorry." Apologizing didn't come easy for him, but he'd say the words as often as he had to. "I was chasing my heart and didn't know it."

Her gaze turned thoughtful. "It seems like I've been chasing my heart for as long as I can remember. I thought I'd found it once, but I was wrong."

"Are you still chasing it?"

"I don't know," she said cautiously. "I may have found it."

What did that mean?

"How will you know?" Four small words, but they may have been the most important he'd ever asked.

"It depends."

"On what?"

Her gaze met his boldly. "On if the man who holds my heart lets me hold his in return."

Was she saying what he thought she was? He framed her face in his hands, caressing her cheeks with his thumbs. "Any man would be a fool to turn you away. I've never thought of myself as a fool, but I've been acting like one lately."

The tentative hope in her eyes was his undoing.

He brushed a kiss across her lips. "You are everything to me," he said when he raised his head. "Even when I couldn't have you, I knew you were the one I'd been dreaming of."

He kissed her again, more deeply this time. "We have a lot of lost time to make up for."

"The time wasn't lost. It was preparing us to know our hearts. Neither of us was ready six years ago to know what we wanted," she said. "Now we are."

He gazed at her in wonder. "Thank you."

"No. Thank the Lord."

Once again, she was right. "I have a lot to learn."

"We both do. We'll do it together. Along with Ruthie and Miso."

"I have a feeling those two will be the ones teaching us."

She laughed softly. "I have a feeling you're right."

He didn't doubt it. Ruthie could run circles around him. "I'll try to keep up."

"Just do your best. That's all I want."

Once more, Brianna had sifted through the clutter of extraneous things and come away with the most important one of all.

"Have I told you that I love you?" he asked.

"Not yet."

"Well, here goes. I love you. I think I've always loved you. That won't stop. Whatever we do, wherever we go, that will never stop."

"Same goes for me."

"I want to promise that we'll have a perfect life together, but I can't. Not if I'm being honest. I'm about as far from perfect as you can get. I can be hardheaded and I like to get my own way. I tend to be messy when I'm involved in a case, and I live on pizza and junk food."

"Perfection is overrated. It's all about the surface and not about what's real."

"You're thinking about Jack."

She nodded. "I had what I thought was the perfect husband and the perfect marriage. It didn't take long for me to learn that it was anything but perfect. Jack looked good on the surface. Underneath, he was shallow and selfish and egotistical. I don't need perfect. I don't *want* perfect. One time, I thought I did. And then I realized it was an illusion.

"I want *real*. I want a real marriage with a family, a big, messy family with laughter and tears and everything else that goes with it. I want a bike in the driveway and Miso winding herself around my legs. And a dog under the table begging for scraps."

She skimmed her knuckles over his jaw. "I want you just as you are. Hardheaded, messy and imperfect."

"What about Ruthie?"

"She already loves you."

"And Miso?" he asked. "Is she ready to accept a male in her all-female household?"

"She'll come around. She's pretty open-minded."

"I hope so," Gideon said fervently. "Because if it's a choice between me and Miso, I know who Ruthie will choose." He had no illusions there.

"We'll just have to make sure that you and Miso become best friends."

He shook his head. "No can do. I already have a best friend." He drew her to him and kissed her tenderly. "You."

"That's the nicest thing anyone's ever said to me." She kissed him back.

"I loved you yesterday," he said. "I love you today. I'll love you tomorrow. And all the to-morrows after that." Tears stung his eyes, but he didn't wipe them away.

"I love you with all that I am, all that I ever hope to be," she said. While he was absorbing the enormity of that, she added, "There's one more thing. Nonnegotiable."

"What's that?" Was that worry in his voice?

"You have to up your pancake game. Orders from Ruthie."

He gave a smart salute. "Anything for Ruthie." He kissed her once again. "And for you. Always."

Ruthie rejoined them at that moment. "Mommy, I have to *go*."

Gideon swung her up in his arms. "How about we get some hot chocolate after a restroom stop?"

She wrapped her arms around his neck. "Mommy and Miso and me love you and want to marry you."

Life didn't get any better.

* * * * *

If you enjoyed Rocky Mountain Vendetta,
*look for these other great books from author
Jane M. Choate, available now:*

Keeping Watch
The Littlest Witness
Shattered Secrets
High-Risk Investigation
Inherited Threat
Stolen Child
Secrets from the Past
Lethal Corruption

*Find more great reads at
www.LoveInspired.com*

Dear Reader,

If you're like me, you've had a rocky two and a half years, with a pandemic raging and all that went with it. Sometimes I wept, asking the Lord to relieve the hardship that many went through and are still going through. Other times, I rejoiced, knowing that the Lord was in charge.

A favorite hymn contains the words "He (the Lord) will guide us through."

The Lord continues to guide me through, just as He did Brianna and Gideon. They endured their own rough moments, with killers after them and painful memories chasing them. But they never gave up.

How many times have I taken the Lord's love for granted? To my shame, too many to count. But He continues to love me, with all my sins and weaknesses. Just as He loves all of us.

The Lord is always there, always guiding us through. And I give thanks.

With faith in His goodness,
Jane

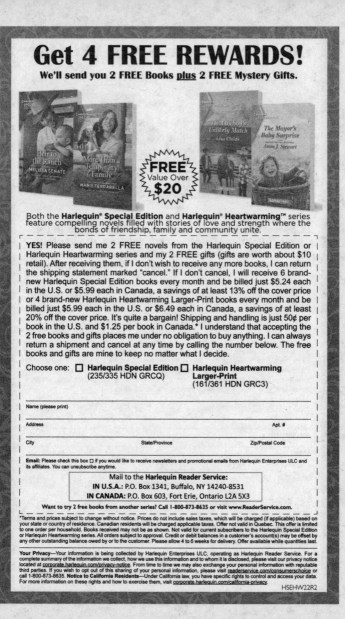

COUNTRY LEGACY COLLECTION

19 FREE BOOKS IN ALL!

EMMETT
Diana Palmer

COURTED BY THE COWBOY

THE RANCHER AND THE BABY
Marie Ferrarella

Cowboys, adventure and romance await you in this new collection! Enjoy superb reading all year long with books by bestselling authors like Diana Palmer, Sasha Summers and Marie Ferrarella!

YES! Please send me the **Country Legacy Collection!** This collection begins with 3 FREE books and 2 FREE gifts in the first shipment. Along with my 3 free books, I'll also get 3 more books from the **Country Legacy Collection**, which I may either return and owe nothing or keep for the low price of $24.60 U.S./$28.12 CDN each plus $2.99 U.S./$7.49 CDN for shipping and handling per shipment*. If I decide to continue, about once a month for 8 months, I will get 6 or 7 more books but will only pay for 4. That means 2 or 3 books in every shipment will be FREE! If I decide to keep the entire collection, I'll have paid for only 32 books because 19 are FREE! I understand that accepting the 3 free books and gifts places me under no obligation to buy anything. I can always return a shipment and cancel at any time. My free books and gifts are mine to keep no matter what I decide.

☐ 275 HCK 1939   ☐ 475 HCK 1939

Name (please print)

Address   Apt. #

City   State/Province   Zip/Postal Code

Mail to the **Harlequin Reader Service:**
IN U.S.A.: P.O. Box 1341, Buffalo, NY 14240-8571
IN CANADA: P.O. Box 603, Fort Erie, Ontario L2A 5X3

50BOOKCL22

HARLEQUIN
PLUS

Announcing a **BRAND-NEW** multimedia subscription service for romance fans like you!

Read, Watch and Play.

Experience the easiest way to get the romance content you crave.

Start your **FREE 7 DAY TRIAL** at www.harlequinplus.com/freetrial.